# Conquest
# of
# Earth

### MANLY BANISTER

AIRMONT

AIRMONT PUBLISHING COMPANY, INC.
22 EAST 60TH STREET · NEW YORK 22

# CONQUEST OF EARTH

An AIRMONT BOOK published by arrangement with
Thomas Bouregy and Company, Inc.

### PRINTING HISTORY

Bouregy edition published June, 1957
Airmont edition published August, 1964

PUBLISHED SIMULTANEOUSLY IN THE DOMINION OF CANADA
BY THE RYERSON PRESS, TORONTO

PRINTED IN THE UNITED STATES OF AMERICA
BY THE COLONIAL PRESS INC., CLINTON, MASSACHUSETTS

# CONTENTS

# 1.  THE INITIATES

After nineteen years, this was the day of days for Kor Danay. As he had expected, the day dawned clear. Almost every day on Earth was clear; as bright as a turgid, blood-red Sun could make it, shining in a dry, cloudless sky that mellowed from almost black at the zenith to a deep indigo at the horizon. In their season, minus-magnitude stars like Sirius and Antares were blazing spicules of light at high noon.

Earth's bare bones, scoured and whitened by desert winds, sucked at the Sun's waning heat, stored it for radiation in the bitter night, when even frost would have softened the cold.

In places, of course, soil, humus, desiccated vegetation, and precious moisture still clung obstinately. People still toiled for their daily bread, and other people enjoyed the cake distributed to them by the Trisz . . . the benevolent Trisz. . . .

Kor lay on the stone-slab floor of his quarters in the Institute of Manhood.

He thought of his first morning at the Institute—when he was six—and he had awakened in this same room, cold, stiff, and tearful. Nineteen years had conditioned childish frailties out of his body. The stone on which he lay was hollowed by the restless movements of generations of learners at the Institute. To sleep on harsh stone was pure luxury, after the training to which the initiate Men were subjected.

It was morning in late spring, with no sign of an impending sandstorm. A fine day, Kor thought, for the Examination which marked his last day at the Institute. There was no such thing as failure of the Examination . . . those who survived it were the ones who did not fail.

From where he lay against the wall, wrapped in his warm blue cloak, Kor could look out through the glassless window opening into the indigo sky.

*Hail the Sun! Lord of creation!* The panegyric phrases drifted through Kor's mind. The Saga of Man had been drilled into him these nineteen years past. Meditation upon its verses was a part of his every action and reaction—a cloak and a shield at once, a cover for the work he was trained to perform. . . .

Kor bounded to his feet, and finished the Awakening Remembrance at the window, in company with Exercises as laid down in Mechanics of Ritual, Section 2A, Subsection D.

His skin was golden . . . it gleamed like reddish brass in the sunlight. His hair was the color of hammered gold. He had gray eyes, lean cheeks, a large nose with flaring nostrils, a full underlip, and a chin slightly rounded.

He raced through the ritual easily, fitting the words and cadences to the smooth, muscular movements of the Exercises. The Remembrances were a recorded whirly-whirl of sounds and nothing more. But here and there, where the tongue tripped over senseless syllables, the mind dwelt upon the semantic interpolations . . . the hidden keys to the power of Manhood.

*Desire is our scourge, and Need is our blessing.* . . . He peered upon his world. A line of poplars tossed in the early breeze. Beyond their screen was the ruffled surface of a small lake.

Precious water! Water was the lifeblood of Earth . . . the fluid that failed now in its subterranean veins and arteries, flowed slowly from the bowels of the earth, to vanish and return no more. Earth's seas soon would be gone. When the Trisz removed the last precious drop . . . Kor straightened his back.

*"Resolve is our armor; Will is our Weapon . . . Belief in our Mission . . . Faith in our Selves . . . . . "*

He raised his arms aloft, hands clasped, and shook them in the ceremonial Sign of the Conqueror.

From a neighboring chamber suddenly came sounds of young men laughing. Water splashed from huge amphors, and ran down carefully chiseled channels and drains in the floor, dripped into the purification tanks in the basement, and returned thence to the supply tanks in the loft. So rare a commodity had to be carefully conserved, no more permitted to evaporate than was absolutely unavoidable.

There was ample water at the Institute; it was in the nature of the inhabitants of the Institute that there should be. It was unfortunate that this plenty could not be made available to the People as well . . . but the secret was one of many which the Institute of Manhood kept from the Trisz —the benevolent Trisz. . . .

"Kor!" bawled a male voice from the door. "Still sleeping? Clean up for the Examination! Would you take all morning to ritualize at the window?"

The six Initiates were the only survivors of the hundred novitiates who had entered the Institute as children, nineteen years before.

Novitiates entering the Institute at the age of six spent six years in physical training and in learning the rudiments of the Philosophy of Man, and Memorizing the Saga. For the following six years, they were termed Students, and received the harshest of physical and mental discipline in their training and studies. Those who proved deficient in physical stamina or mental acumen were transferred to regularization classes for further training, leading to initiation into the Order of the Blue Brothers. The Blue Brothers were an order of the highest significance, the Guides and Protectors of the People. The Blue Brothers were the graduate Teachers of Earth.

Few were the Students accepted into the Order of Initiates, where seven years of specialized training fitted them for the Order of the Men. This was the prime purpose of the Institute—to select and train candidates for the Men . . . the Scarlet Sages. Their deepest mysteries were known only to those who personally were weavers of the scarlet cloak.

*To be a Man is Greatness . . . it is Nobility . . .* thought Kor Danay.

Earth was incredibly ancient. Millions of generations of the People had come and gone upon its withering surface . . . There was no actual historical record of when the Trisz had first come to Earth.

That was what the People called them—Trisz. The Conquerors had no name of their own. The world of sound was closed to the Trisz. They ruled the People and never heard them speak.

Kor Danay had never seen a Trisz, not even a picture of one. No picture could have portrayed the Trisz. They looked as their name sounds—their appearance an illusory refraction of light, as the morning wind upon the Institute lake.

Kor could afford to be leisurely with his dressing. There would be no breakfast for the examinees this morning. Nor was fast to be broken until the Sun had set upon the day of Examination.

Keeping the fast was ritual, as the Examination was ritual. No Man could fail this Examination, except that he destroyed himself fulfilling the requirements.

For the last time, Kor drew on the blue regalia of the Institute—silken blue hose of gossamer woven plastic, blue leather buskins that wrapped up his claves, jerkin of blue leather, sleeveless and laced at the front. Finally, Kor threw over his shoulders the rippling cloak of the Wearers of the Blue, the same garment worn by the Blue Brotherhood, but embroidered wth the deeper-toned insignia of the Institute—uplifted hands clasped in the Sign of the Conqueror. The next time he dressed, his color would be scarlet.

Only the Outlanders of Earth bore arms—thin, rapier-like weapons or daggers. Anything more dangerous was forbidden by the Trisz, except for the troops of the regional Lords, who handled sword, spear, and bow with equal facility. The terrible energy weapons of the Trisz were prohibited, reserved exclusively for the elite city guards of Triszmen.

Weaponless, therefore, Kor entered the hall. The class marched out of the building, across a rippling sward of blue grass and into the arena where the Masters of Examination awaited them.


Things had been different in antiquity, Kor knew. He could not be sure how different, or in what way. History passed back across two Ages of Ice, and before that it was very, very dim. It was said in their texts—though taken with a grain of salt in these enlightened times—that once all of the People had called themselves Men. It was certain that none of them had *been* Men. To be a Man was a special privilege and a product of arduous training of mind and body. It was not generally believed, that any before the latter-day Men possessed the kind of minds the Men had, nor even their physical attributes.

The Men were suffered by the Trisz to exist as an ancient institution that brought guidance to the People. Nominally, the Men were the spiritual leaders of the People, including the Triszmen—though the latter naturally owed their allegiance to the Trisz, and not to the authority of a regional lord.

The sociological aspect of this latter-day Earth was a peculiar one . . . The Trisz were on top, then the Triszmen, and at the bottom—the People. Although Kor had not traveled, physically, so much as a yard into the world beyond the limits of the Institute, it was necessary that he be kept informed in order to re-enter it at the conclusion of his training.

It was not only the thought of his pending return that sent a shudder of anticipation through Kor. He had a secret of his own; one which he felt was of great importance to every Man, and ultimately, to the People and to Earth. To-day's examination would reveal that specialized ability the young Initiate had assiduously practiced in his years of study and drill.

The Men had developed the highest type of double mind in the Universe—a mind that gave them complete mastery of their environment to the nth degree. So far, only Kor Danay knew that his own mind, developing a latent function peculiar to itself, had gone beyond even the far-reaching mental development of the Men. Kor's was not only a double, but a separable mind.

The Initiates stood stiffly at attention before the rostrum erected in the center of the athletic field. The green-clad elder Men, who were the Masters, stood grouped upon the stand, murmuring last-minute details among themselves.

Val Shan, Supreme Master of the Institute, faced the junior Men below. His was an imposing figure. Val Shan was over two centuries old, but he appeared not over fifty, as age is recognized among the People.

"Men . . ." His words came slowly and clearly. "You are the one hundred sixty-first class I have helped graduate from the Institute." He smiled gravely. "I was assistant instructor at the first graduation I attended functionally. There were two Men in that class. There are six in this . . . the largest class ever graduated at one time by any of the Institutes."

Kor flung his glance around the empty, tiered stone seats of the Arena. A week ago the Blue Brothers had conducted their ceremony here and then had gone out to their Lodges in the world of the People. He had watched that graduation. But there were no spectators for this one. A special force field now surrounded the entire area, effectively preventing entry even by the Trisz.

". . . You have been impressed with the fact that your training has been conducted in secret," Val Shan continued clearly. "No one outside the Brotherhood of Men knows of your training, your capabilities, or your aims. You know what you have been trained for—the world does not. The

9

welfare of the People is in your charge . . . your work is for them, regardless of how they, in their ignorance, may work against you.

"It has been said that once, in ages before the Trisz, the world was peopled only by the race of Man. Earth shall again become a world of Men alone. The people are our sacred trust. To free them and Earth of the Trisz and to lift the People again to the stature of Men is our sworn and solemn duty."

Val Shan concluded his brief speech, announced the order of the Examination, and turned the procedure over to a junior Master.

First came the Games, followed by the Contests. The Initiates contended with each other, in pairs and in groups. The Games tested their manual skill, their co-ordination of mind and muscle. In the Contests, they pitted themselves against each other in wrestling, boxing, fencing, racing, and jumping.

After a period of relaxation, Val Shan called Kor to the rostrum.

"Are you ready for your first Challenge?"

Kor Danay nodded stiffly. "Yes, Sir."

"Good. I can tell you nothing about your problem in advance. The Challenges have been carefully thought out, and are the result of centuries of experiment. They are intended to bring out the best you have at your command. You have ten seconds in which to adjust your mind to the first Challenge."

## 2.   THE TESTING OF KOR

Kor Danay staggered in slippery ooze. The exchange had been appallingly swift . . . instantaneous.

Around him, primeval ferns hurled fronded tops into low-lying mist. Rotting humus, watery wastescape cloyed at his nostrils.

Off to his right, something began to splash heavily in the streaming mists. A struggle was taking place between unseen, monstrous beasts of this primeval world. Kor's conscious mind was aware of the tumult; his superconscious mind quivered with anticipation of something else, picked up the calm voice of Val Shan, speaking in tones of infinite calm.

"Kor, you have been transported to a young planet, located somewhere in your own galaxy. I may not give you its galactic co-ordinates. It will be your Challenge to return to us here on Earth . . . to the exact spot in the arena from which you were transported. The time allowed for this is three point two seconds. You will be credited with five points if you return in this time, ten points if in less, two-and-a-half points if more. A return to any point in the Solar System, requiring reorientation for the final return is worth only two points . . . two-and-a-half points for a similar return elsewhere on Earth. Time begins when you hear the pseudosound of the gong."

The Master spoke only in Kor's superconscious mind, the marvelous instrument forged in the training of the Men. Far away . . . it seemed to him that a muted gong chimed melodiously. He had 3.2 seconds in which to orientate himself, select the swiftest orbit home, and to appear before the Masters in the arena.

The simplest Challenges came first, of course.

Silence flashed across the primitive world. Ferns and rippled marsh-ponds presented an appearance of frozen, stroboscopic rigidity. It seemed as if Time had suddenly fled from this world.

His training had stressed speed of reaction. His double, separable mind automatically assumed control of its environment. Kor was living fast now, so fast that he could grow old and die before Val Shan could step down from the rostrum.

Time was a matter of how you were adjusted to it, Kor thought fleetingly, satisfied with the immediate response of his superconscious mind. It only seemed that a stasis of time seized the surroundings. Actually, every electron in his body vibrated at a tremendous cyclic rate, speeding up his perception of time. His body was matter beyond matter, wholly subject to his own will . . . cast completely out of the time-rate of the Universe.

"*Desire is our scourge . . .*" Kor thought, arrowing upward through the now-solid mists that shrouded this world. A high-cycle passage opened ahead of him as he forged through and out of the atmosphere, into the vacuum of space. "*Need is our blessing. . . .*" The planet was a golden disc, distant in space. Stars glittered with cold fury in far immensities.

He checked their alignment and distribution with a cold, reasoning analysis. It was impossible to recognize their ap-

11

pearance, or to attempt a spectral analysis while he was in this state of time-stasis. The light which reached his senses was distorted, stepped up in its own cyclic rate of vibration. Analysis of the starlight could tell him nothing.

Kor Danay drifted in timelessness. There was neither heat nor cold in this state. Airlessness was a condition without meaning. No longer matter in the accepted sense, his body did not require oxygen or pressure. It drew its furious needs from the inexhaustible store of sub-etheric energy tapped by his mind.

He relaxed and let his mind expand.

Impressions poured through to him. Matter . . . here, there, everywhere . . . planets, suns, aimlessly drifting planetoids. He searched more widely, receiving, sorting, classifying. Three thousand-odd light years away, a familiar, low buzz caught his attention. He mentalized a shift in the time-warp that held him and thrilled to the momentary, excited *chirp-chirp-chirp* into which the signal developed.

Again Kor shifted the lever of his conscious mind against his superconsciousness. The Universe blacked out. He shifted once more, sorting, seeking, classifying, rejecting . . . Out of the darkness sprang the tiered stone seats of the arena, the assembled Examination Masters. Val Shan stood on the rostrum, holding an electronic stop watch. He drew in a slow breath. His nostrils dilated as he smiled with a pleased expression.

"One point oh three seconds, Kor. You have done well!"

The Initiates went through their Challenges singly, Kor with mounting excitement as the ease and speed of his accomplishments dazzled even himself.

Finally, the long day of Challenges drew to a close. The Sun cast long shadows across the floor of the arena. Val Shan held up his hand.

"The Examination is concluded," he said. "However," he continued in his calm, peaceful voice, "at this point in the Examination, opportunity is given the Initiates to demonstrate what has romantically been called the Fire Out of Heaven. You have studied its laws, and you are aware of what it means, but no Man has ever successfully controlled the Fire. To attempt to control it and to fail means instant, sure destruction.

"You are cautioned to think carefully before volunteering to attempt such a demonstration. You will be required to demonstrate separately, in remote sections of the galaxy from each other, for the action must take place far from the usual trade lanes of the Trisz. A Master will accompany each Initiate for the purpose of observing the Challenge. If none of you choose to demonstrate, that is well. It is possible that no mind will ever learn to control the Fire."

Quiet settled over the arena. Kor Danay lifted his hand. "Sir . . . I should like to demonstrate the Challenge!"

Val Shan nodded. "Very well."

Jon Moran spoke up. "And I, Sir!"

"Any others?" Val Shan roved his calm gaze over the Initiates. No other volunteered. "That is good. You others may return to your quarters and prepare for the ceremonial breaking of fast."

Kor's heart thudded painfully as the four Initiates filed out of the arena. Would he ever see them again? Jon Moran lifted clasped hands in the ceremonial Sign of the Conqueror and grinned at him. Kor grinned in return, lifted his own hands in the Sign.

"Val Shan," Kor said, "I should like your company at the Challenge."

The Master inclined his head in acknowledgment.

It was dark as the eternal night of Space on the planet to which Val Shan took himself and Kor Danay. The surface was a frozen rubble of volcanic ash and great, tumbled slabs of glassy obsidian. Almost directly overhead, a singular star blazed with the intensity of a carbon arc—the far-off sun of this abysmal and nighted planet.

There was no air to breathe. Their bodies vibrated in time-stasis. Kor touched his mind to that of the Master. "Sir . . . yonder is a high mountain. Please retire to its summit for your personal safety. Break all mental contact with me, for I must work alone."

"How can I observe if I do not hold contact with you? If your demonstration should fail, I must be in a position to learn."

"No! I have worked out all the equations on the cybernograph, Sir, and I believe that there is something in the additional mind which introduces an aberration."

"Kor, have you performed the demonstration in secret?"

"Yes, Sir. I have drawn the Fire Out of Heaven!"

"Very well. I withdraw."

Val Shan retired to the mountain top as directed. He watched the desolate plain where Kor Danay stood, but Kor knew that he could not be seen by the sense of physical sight alone. What he was about to do would be seen, though.

He looked down. His conscious mind floated miles above the glassy, ash-covered plain. He perceived himself far below, poised like an athlete. He sensed the mighty effort of mind that went into the drawing together of universal forces. The figure of himself staggered with strain. Kor Danay was wholly divorced from that figure; he was only an observer.

This was the crux of his secret, this ability of his to separate the twin factors of his mind. The presence of even his own ego in the performance of this task introduced aberrations into the elaborate forces of mind which wove and rewove in his superconsciousness. His separable mind was the answer to the problem.

Kor's superconsciousness drove like a physical thing across the gap of space to the sun of this peopleless world. It was only by virtue of supraliminal perception that he was aware of what occurred on that seething surface, the violence of the storms that began to rage in its atmosphere. A whirlpool of energy was drawn upward from the surface, controlled and directed by the power of the Initiate's unleashed mind.

The lonely, wooden figure on the airless plain moved stiffly. Its arm rose, hurled forward . . . and a river of scarlet flame gushed across the eerie landscape. Volcanic upthrusts, frozen for an eternity in the endless chill of space, showered sparks, toppled, melted into magma and flowed in the torrent of flame.

The scene blotted out. Kor Danay and Val Shan stood again in the arena of the Institute of Manhood on Earth.

"You could smash the Solar System with that power," the Master observed calmly, but it was apparent that he restrained himself with difficulty.


## 3.   "BEWARE, O TRISZ . . ."


The ceremonial breakfast was conducted in silence, for only five graduates were on hand. Jon Moran had not returned, nor had the Master who accompanied him.

Concluding the meal, the graduates returned to their quarters to don the scarlet garments that had been laid out for them in their absence. They were now entitled to wear the regalia of Men.

Kor Danay sought to dull the ache of grieving for his friend. *Resolve is our armor; Will is our weapon.* . . . He murmured the ritualistic babble, seeking comfort in its hidden interpolations.

In the Audience Hall of the Administration Building, the Masters awaited the graduate classmen. The latter filed in, splendid-looking in their garments and robes of scarlet, and took places close to the front.

Val Shan rose. "Men . . ." He welcomed them into the Brotherhood, spoke briefly on their scholastic records, then went on, "What I have to tell you now will be received sadly by you. You will wonder why you have been required to attain to the lengths you have, why you have learned to control the vast powers of your minds, when it is possible that none of you will ever be permitted to use those powers."

He paused to let his words sink in. Kor heard the sound of the words, but their import did not strike him at once. When it did, he felt himself tighten inside.

"You are about to be given the Oath of Manhood," Val Shan continued evenly. "You are expected to obey its conditions. There are sound reasons behind the Oath—it will be easy to see why it is necessary, but not so easy to see how you can live up to it. But live up to it you must, if the Brotherhood of Men is to survive and reach its goal. Stand up, now, and repeat the Oath after me."

The five stood up mechanically, held clasped hands aloft, and repeated the phrases of the ritual Oath after Val Shan.

"I do solemnly vow . . . never in vanity or in pride . . . to demonstrate my powers . . . to any living thing . . . nor to use my powers against any of the People . . . except that my life be in danger . . . nor against any of the Trisz. This I most solemnly swear . . . that I will face death before the Trisz . . . and will let my life be lost . . . rather than disclose the secret powers of the Men to them. I sanctify myself . . . in the service of Earth . . . in the race of People and Men. I accept my responsibilities in the world as a minister of spiritual comfort . . . and promise to discharge my duties as befits a Man . . . to hold the chapter sacred and inviolate . . . and the Lodge of my body . . . I shall keep chaste and pure . . . for the space of one year from this graduation . . ."

There was more—much more. Kor intoned the words dismally, feeling that he had been cheated, if not robbed.

Why those nineteen years, just to become a Teacher? But Men could not teach truth to the People without revealing their own true nature to the Trisz. That was why they deliberately clung to the Philosophy, why the Blue Brotherhood were trained to expound it learnedly, in full belief of its truth. The Philosophy was the only contact the Men had with all the People, for Philosophy was the only universal contact permitted by the Trisz.

Val Shan explained these things after the formula had been recited. A foolish demonstration of their powers would awaken the Trisz to danger. They would be sure to retaliate with an endeavor to wipe out the Men. And that could be done, Val Shan assured them.

Their role as guides and protectors of the People was enhanced by the prohibition contained in the Oath, for the People of Earth were unorganized—divided into hundreds of restless tribes that warred among themselves. A Man who permitted himself to be swayed by regional jealousies to the point of taking part in these internecine struggles could succeed only in revealing the nature and purpose of the Brotherhood to the Trisz, who not only condoned these wars among their subjects, but actually encouraged them.

It all revolved around the same theme—the specialized powers of the Men must not be revealed.

"The Trisz are a totally alien life form," Val Shan explained. "No one knows how many Trisz there are, or if the Trisz might be only one. We know that the Trisz is a self-contained energy-form, which does not explain them at all. We do know this, though, that even if there are many Trisz, it is as if there were only one. It is believed that somewhere in the Universe there is a planet inhabited by the parent body, to which all Trisz are anchored by hyperspatial filaments of mind. Therefore, what one Trisz may observe is instantly known to all Trisz everywhere throughout the Universe, a local Trisz being merely an extension of the parent body.

"You see, then, how impossible it would be to destroy the Trisz one at a time. In order to do so, we must find the Trisz' home planet and destroy it entirely with the parent body. Until we do find that planet, we must take extreme care."

Slowly, Kor Danay's understanding grasped a mental picture of a vast world whirling through space in some remote island universe—a distant and unknown galaxy. Men secretly combed the reaches of space for that home of the

Trisz, Val Shan told them, and hinted at further secret activities of the Men, but firmly closed his lips upon all details.

He abruptly changed the subject and spoke glowingly of Kor's accomplishment, his drawing the Fire Out of Heaven. But his voice was sad as he confessed that the ability was Kor's alone because, to his knowledge, only Kor Danay had the unique type of separable mind that seemed to be required. It might take centuries to adapt Men to the separable kind of intelligence which Kor resorted to instinctively.

Val Shan brightened suddenly and spoke fondly to them. "Someday, however, Men shall prevail over the Trisz. Perhaps you very Men. Therefore, I bid you farewell with love and with hope for the future. In the morning each will receive his assignment and will be dispatched to duty in the world of the People and the Trisz. Return now to your quarters."

It was not so much that Kor resented his assignment to No-ka-si, the human settlement adjacent to the Trisz stronghold of Ka-si. He had at least hoped for preferential treatment because of his handiness with the Fire Out of Heaven. After all, did he not know about the Searchers who combed space for the lair of the Trisz? His own father had been one of them, had given his life in the search.

If any Man deserved an honorable post of hair-raising adventure, Kor thought, surely he was that Man. Val Shan sympathized with his views.

"There is an ancient saying," he observed with deep calm, "to the effect that he also serves who only stands and waits. Be patient, my son. The life of a Man is long. I myself have seen more than ten generations of the People. No excuse has yet been found for not living to the end of Time —except accident. The Men are somehow . . . prone to accident."

He tugged at his chin thoughtfully. "You know our methods of extrapolation. Have you extrapolated your own future yet?"

"I hadn't thought of it," Kor confessed. "The practice always seemed a little confusing to me, and of little value. We used to play at it, as Initiates, but one day was much like the next and we soon tired of it."

"Let me tell you something," Val Shan said seriously. "It is a faculty you would do well to cultivate. We must strive constantly to be the equal of the Trisz, if not their better.

Many of the things which you have been taught would be considered miracles by the People, but familiar mind-mechanics to the Trisz. In many things we barely match their ability. In others—you especially in regard to the Fire—we outmatch them. In still others, they are our masters. Extrapolation, for instance."

"The Trisz extrapolate?"

"They have machines which extrapolate for them. That is why you are being sent to No-ka-si.

"You have learned something of the social order of the People and the Trisz," the old Master went on. "You have been shown how the Trisz rule through internal disruption of human civilization. The culture of the People of today is at a lower level than ever before during the tenure of the Trisz. The People are divided into small, regional units, communications stifled, rivalries bred, education impeded. Human civilization has been swiftly moving backward. When I was a boy, steam locomotives still were in use on this continent. Today, the horse and wagon have replaced it in the long-distance transportation of freight and passengers.

"As a Man, you are familiar with the brilliant technology of the Men. This technology rivals that of the Trisz; we know, because we are familiar with the ways of the Trisz. Our technology has made your training possible by effectively canceling out the inquisitive spy-rays of the Trisz, which are always focused on the Institutes throughout the world. It would not have been enough merely to shield ourselves from the spy-rays; we cannot even let the Trisz know that we are able to shield ourselves from his rays. We impress upon his spy-beams, therefore, recorded scenes of the kind we want the Trisz to view—giving an entirely false picture of the Institute.

"To the Trisz, therefore—and it goes without saying, to the Triszmen as well—we are only a sect of bookish pedants." He laughed shortly. "Suspicion is the prime virtue of the tyrant. The Trisz rule upon thousands—if not millions—of worlds where they are considerably less than welcome. They maintain their position solely through nourishing the kind of suspicion that calls for eternal watchfulness.

"The Trisz are a race unto themselves, completely alien. And we are as alien to them as they are to us. It is a feat of reason to be able to outguess your own species. To outguess an alien is an extremely difficult mental exercise. To help themselves outguess us, the Trisz long ago developed a machine, a super-extension of our electronic cybernograph. One is installed in every principal Trisz city on Earth, and in every similar location in the Universe.

"It is called the Extrapolator. Its diet is a daily stream of sociological data that keeps its mechanical 'mind' stuffed with the latest concerns and affairs of each district. The brain of the machine sorts, classifies, and evaluates all such data and files it in its memory sectors. When quesions concerning the future trend of events are put to the machine, it is enabled to draw remarkably shrewd conclusions that amount to an ability actually to foretell the future."

"This machine must be important to me," the young Sage observed, "or you would not tell me about it."

Val Shan smiled. "The Ka-si Extrapolator has predicted you, Kor."

"Sir!"

"We have our spies—we know almost everything we wish to know about the Trisz. Our spies lurk among the Triszmen—human beings who have sold themselves for hire to the conqueror. Unfortunately, most of these slaves—these Triszmen—love their chains. They offer allegiance to the Trisz for the privileges the Trisz offer them. It is chiefly these you will need to be cautious of in the world. You will have to learn to anticipate them in order to live long."

Kor interrupted. "How could the machine have predicted *me*?"

Val Shan shrugged. "It is only obvious to us that the machine has done so. Kor, you objected once to the confusing aspect of our method of extrapolation. The Extrapolator seems to have its own difficulties on this same score. It never makes a forthright statement that such-and-such is bound to occur at a given time. It couches its conclusions in symbolic, almost mystic terms, something like the oracles which tradition says spoke to the People in the hidden past.

"The Trisz present the problem of a local uprising to their machine as a continuing routine check. Many times the prediction given by the Extrapolator has resulted in smashing minor local defections of officials, has shown up petty embezzlements, chicaneries, or a troublesome feud. The machine has so far proved its value to the Trisz. They will hardly overlook its latest pronouncement relating to Ka-si."

"That is—?"

" 'Beware, O Trisz, the Scarlet Sage to come, for then

*shall danger rage,' "* quoted Val Shan. "I told you the utterance of the machine tends toward the mystic or symbolic. The Men are called Scarlet Sages by the People. This local chapter at Ka-si has been recently vacated. A new Man is required in the position. Therefore, you must be the one to go to Ka-si."

"The future is difficult to predict because it can be changed," Kor Danay observed. "If you should send me to Nwok or Lun—what then?"

"Of course the future can be changed," Val Shan nodded agreement. "Prescience affords the opportunity to introduce aberrating factors into the trend of events. But there are three reasons, at least, why we don't want to change this prediction, Kor. First, to send another Man than yourself would be to endanger his life uselessly. The Trisz are alerted by their Extrapolator, and they would destroy him. His oath would leave him helpless to defend himself. Second, if another Man were sent, you may be sure the Trisz would investigate him thoroughly. If they should find that he was indeed no danger to them, they would suspect us of introducing an aberrant. You can see where that would lead. And third, Kor, we are very anxious to follow this probability to its end. We should like to see, if you will, just how dangerous you can be to the Trisz—and still live!"

## 4. THE TRAP

The carriage was a miserable conveyance. A pot-bellied diligence style, it had high iron-shod wheels that bumped and ground across the parched plains of ancient Kansas. The hoofs of the four-horse team thudded dispiritedly. The desiccated vehicle groaned a wretched protest in every joint and rivet. Over the perpetual jangle of harness, the driver from his box above shouted a periodic "Hoo-up!" and sharply cracked his whip.

The carriage was covered with bags, boxes, and bales—piled on the roof and lashed on behind. Dust covered everything.

Kor Danay huddled inside, crowded among a half-dozen other passengers who sat facing each other on hard board seats that ran athwart the carriage. Two of the passengers were Triszmen, accompanied by a woman. The other three

were Outlanders, dressed in dull, brownish garb. The Triszmen wore the saffron cloaks of their station. Their garments were of fine texture, now sadly the worse for grime
and wear.

Kor studied them thoughtfully, so far as he could without appearing curious. Both were men in their early thirties,
the woman a few years younger, perhaps. The woman sat
between them, looking at neither, seeming to interest herself in the never-changing wastescape visible through the
narrow carriage windows.

Wind from an inferno spat through the openings, hurled
stinging particles of sand with its furious breath. The heat
was terrific.

No one talked. It was obvious to Kor that these Triszmen, who had got on at the last overnight stop, had other
things on their mind than conversation. Two of the Outlanders shared the board seat with him; the other crouched
on the weaving floor, clutching a dirty bundle of what appeared to be old rags.

Kor Danay was not used to enduring such common
physcal hardship as this. Ordinarily, he could easily have
made proper compensation for the heat and roughness of
traveling—a minor adjustment of his mind would have
taken care of it nicely—except that he dared not appear as
a picture of cool comfort before his miserable companions.
They rode unashamed of their sweat, grime, and aching
muscles. To avoid seeming other than human, Kor had to
sweat it out with them. He did so, grimly.

"Perhaps," he finally suggested aloud, "we could make
this trip more enjoyable. Has anybody got any ideas?"

The Outlanders eyed each other with embarrassment.
The Triszmen remained wrapped in their cloaks. The
woman scowled out the open window.

"We might sing a few songs," Kor murmured.

The Outlander on the floor moved cramped legs, rolled
over on his bundle of dirty rags. "I ain't much of a hand to
sing, Master, but maybe some of these others . . ."

The Outlander at the Sage's left grinned. "I can't sing
without my bottle of synth, and the way these land travel
companies charge for baggage, I couldn't afford to bring it
along!"

The other Outlander maintained a somber silence.

Kor lifted his gaze to the young woman across from him.
"Perhaps the young lady could suggest something."

One of the Triszmen unwrapped a fold of cloak from his

face. One eye peered out balefully. "She doesn't sing, Master."

The girl shot a beseeching glance at Kor. He would have given a great deal to look into her mind just then, but indiscriminate mind-tapping was prohibited by the Brotherhood. It was impossible to do it without being detected.

The sun stood high as the carriage finally pulled off the road among a clump of cottonwoods. The road twisted and turned among low hills, following a small stream that wound among scrubby trees before losing itself farther on in the desert sands. At this particular point, the stream had been widened and deepened to make a watering place.

The carriage door swung open and the driver barked at them: "Hour stop. Lunch. Water the horses. All out!"

It was good to stretch one's legs in the open. Kor walked briskly up and down, performing the ceremonial Exercises of the Men. The Outlanders had retired to the shade of a cottonwood. The bundle of rags held by one turned out to be a lunch for all three. The Triszmen and their woman companion had disappeared.

Kor walked around the carriage curiously, but there was no one on the other side. It was quiet in the oasis, except for the far splashing of the horses in the stream.

He was about to round the rear of the coach, when the sound of rapid footsteps drew him back. He turned. The young woman hurried toward him from the far side of the road.

"Master! Learned Sir!"

She was breathing heavily. "You must stop them!" she gasped. "They are fighting!"

"Who are fighting, lady?"

"My husband and my brother. You must stop them!"

She started back, gesturing quickly. Kor paused, alert. He dared use his mind here. A hundred yards away, in a small draw, he sensed two men crouching motionless. *Fighting?*

"Peace!" he commanded quietly. "It is not proper for a man of guidance to intervene in family affairs. Why are they fighting?"

The woman wrung her hands. Tears stood in her eyes. "Please. They will kill each other!"

"Why are they fighting?"

She began to sob. "I left my husband and returned to my family, but my husband came to get me. My family would not give me up, only consenting upon my husband's promise to be good to me in the future. My brother accompanies us back to the city to be sure that conditions are now as my husband promises. They got into another argument. But please hurry, Sir—before one should hurt the other!"

Her story, oustide its vagueness, was full of flaws. If she were an Outlander, then her brother was an Outlander also. Why, therefore, did he wear the clothing of a Triszman? He decided to see.

"Very well. I will go with you."

The Triszmen still crouched motionless, but as Kor and the woman approached, he heard the sudden ring of steel on steel. One shouted an oath.

The two were going heavily at it in the draw, slashing and thrusting with their weapons. Kor almost smiled at the thought that either could harm the other with their faked thrusts and feints.

"Hurry! Hurry!" the woman cried.

"You can see that I am unarmed," he pointed out, keeping a wary eye on the fencers. Their footwork was execrable, their stance utterly impossible.

"Speak to them, Sir!"

"Very well, if that will do."

He strode toward the slashing pair. "Ho—you two!"

Neither combatant paid him the slightest attention. The air was curdled around them with the sulphurous utterance of oaths.

"Stop your fighting!" Kor shouted. "I command you to be at peace!"

Both Triszmen whirled at once, teeth showing in grins. One ran at him, blade leveled. "Kill the Scarlet Sage!"

How stupid of them, Kor thought, to believe they could kill him. He had already mentally detected the energy weapon in the other Triszman's belt. As the fellow drew his weapon, depending on the swordsman to keep the Sage distracted, Kor Danay nullified its charge with a simple shift of electrons. He side-stepped the lunge of the advancing swordsman, seized that worthy by the arm, whirled, and flung him at his fellow conspirator.

The two sprawled on the sandy ground, rolled over, leaped up and started running. The woman was already clawing her way up the steep side of the draw. In a moment, all three were out of sight.

"A very clumsy maneuver," Kor pondered. "I wonder why."

It took only a moment to locate the trio. Three horses had been tethered in the next ravine, and the conspirators were already mounted and riding like mad.

The Sage smiled faintly, tossed the unretrieved rapiers behind a boulder, and returned to the coach to while away the remainder of the noon hour. He had not provided himself with lunch since food was not a necessity when he chose to do without it.

The missing Triszmen caused a little delay while the driver swore, apologized, fumed, and sent the Outlanders to look for them. The Outlanders came back empty-handed.

"If they like it here," growled the driver, "they can just stay—if they haven't been picked up by a band of Roamers. This country is full of 'em!"

The thought of Roamers—outlaw wanderers of the wastelands—spurred the driver to furious action. He got the remainder of his passengers aboard quickly, leaped to his box and whipped the horses into a plunging gallop down the road.

Most of Earth was burning desert in these latter days, and this part of the world was no exception.

Kor was more than pleased that the Trisz had already moved against him. He kept alert, but no further incident occurred to unsettle his tranquillity.

For days, the coach staggered and ground along the dusty way, changing horses at convenient stops, discharging and taking on passengers. Mostly, they were the natural inhabitants of these desert plains. Some were obviously journeying from distant parts, but no more came dressed as Triszmen.

Nights were passed at cheerless inns along the forbidding route. These inns were maintained by the land travelers associations that ran the coach lines, and were supported by the outrageous toll exacted.

It neared sunset, a day's travel from the city of the Trisz. The coach shuddered to a creaking stop in an inn courtyard. Stiff, weary passengers climbed down. Kor sighed. A simple "twist" of his mind, and he could have journeyed almost instantaneously to Ka-si.

The stuffy air of the inn reeked of stale food, spilled synthetics, sweat, and grime. For appearances' sake, the Sage ate a meager supper of stewed meat and a buttery synthetic, then retired to his room.

As usual, he slept on the floor. After nineteen years of sleeping on the stone floor of his Institute chamber, he could not be conditioned, even by a coach ride, to try sleeping in a soft bed.

He awoke in the still dark of the night.

His extrasensory perception functioned, dispelling the dark. He sensed a Person—a man of the People—leaning above the bed, feeling cautiously over the quilts with his left hand. The intruder's other hand held a long, sharp knife.

Kor had not seen this fellow before in his travels, but had noticed him last night at the bar of the inn, swilling synthetic alcohol.

The Person was small, poorly dressed. He looked hungry. Just now, he had thin lips drawn back from wolfish-looking teeth as he pawed for the body he expected to find lying there.

Kor raised himself on his elbow. "Are you looking for someone, friend?"

The Triszman—obviously such, in spite of his poor dress—whirled with an expression of fear and consternation. He held the knife uplifted as if to ward off attack.

"You seem disturbed that I am not asleep in my bed," Kor observed. "May I ask t what I owe the honor of this visit?"

The Person made gulping, strangled sounds and began to edge toward the window.

"You cannot move," Kor told him. "Please answer my question."

The intruder stiffened. His face lost all expression. "I came here to kill you," he said.

"Why?"

"I kill for hire."

"You mean you have no reason to dislike me?"

"No."

"Yet you would kill me?"

"Yes."

"Again, why?"

"For the money. He offered to pay me well."

Kor nodded in the dark and pushed easily into the Person's mind. It was something he had to do, to avoid killing the fellow. And he would have to cover his action afterward. He sorted through the memories, for the most part obscured by what obviously was synth-addiction. Finally he extracted the image he sought . . . He perceived the saintly looking face of a fleshy, middle-aged man garbed in blue.

"Is this the one who hired you?"

"Yes. He is a Wearer of the Blue."

Kor lifted his eyebrows. "His name?"

"I do not know."

"What is his Lodge?"

"I don't know that, either."

"Very well." Kor carefully memorized the features of the Blue Brother. "Who knows you are in my room?"

"Nobody knows. I took a room here three days ago. I have been waiting for you to come."

"You know, don't you, that it is a serious crime to attempt the life of a Scarlet Sage?"

"I know it is."

Kor thought carefully. He must move with care to avoid showing his own hand. Naturally, the Person's mission must fail, but how could he make that failure appear natural?

The tenor of the fellow's memories provided a clue. "You are in need of money?"

"Yes."

"You have received Guidance at a Lodge?"

"Yes."

Kor smiled. "Then you know that the Scarlet Sages forgive the misdeeds of people who repent. If you are sorry, repeat the remembrances after me." There was no doubt that the Person would take this opportunity. His mumble echoed Kor Danay's words: "There is hope for the erring as well as the upright. None is held guilty who repents in his heart . . ."

The assassin fell on the floor and moaned, hands over his face. Obviously he had encountered some of the "miracles" of the Blue Brothers in the past, if not of the Sages.

"Arise," Kor said kindly. "You are forgiven. In token of your forgiveness . . . do you know how to make the Sign of the Conqueror?"

The prostrate person whimpered, "Yes."

"Arise and make it. As an earnest of my forgiveness, your clasped and lifted hands will glow with the glory of the upright."

The fellow got to his feet, lifted clasped hands in the Sign. A faint glow quickly brightened and grew into a blaze of supernal light that flooded the room with a naked glare.

A look of ecstasy turned the rat-like little features of the man into a picture of weird beauty.

"Go in peace," Kor told him gently. "Tell all whom you meet of the glory you have witnessed."

That was enough, Kor decided. He had broken a minor rule of the Brotherhood, but he had not broken his Oath. Proselytizing by mental impression was a forbidden practice, but it was a lesser evil than murdering the unfortunate fellow.

He hoped the incident would distress the Trisz, at the same time that it would appear aliently normal to them. Not professing to understand human superstition, the Trisz tolerated it as a useful instrument for holding the People in check.

## 5. KA-SI

The Trisz city of Ka-si was built on the bluffs above the ancient, bone-dry bed of the river Miz-zou. The desert swept in from the western plains, a sea of sand that lapped at the spired mound of the city and flowed eastward almost to Set-loo, where the Mis-pi still trickled southward in a scanty flow to the shrunken sea.

Accustomed as he was to the irrigated greenness of the Institute surroundings in the mountains, Kor Danay still found strange beauty in the wind-swept wastes that pressed in upon the city. Overhead, the cloudless bowl of indigo minimized the half-mile-high reach of city spires, sungleaming in brilliant contrast against the sky.

Once, he knew, the sky had been not indigo, but as blue as the robes of the Brothers. Water vapor had clustered then in cottony gobbets high in the upper air, and the sun had shone bright yellow upon a land that was everywhere lush and verdant.

It still rained upon Earth, but not often in most places, and in many places never. The Sun was swollen and old, and the waters of the planet were dissipated. Earth struggled in her last days. Soon, she would be dead, and her People with her, and her Men, and every last living thing under the Sun. Because of the Trisz.

History implied that Earth was still green when the Trisz first came. Her oceans had been filled with cubic miles of precious water. But slowly, over thousands of years, the Trisz had deliberately sapped the planet. Nobody knew exactly why or how, but the best observations of the Men had long ago led them to believe that the Trisz converted Earth's water into energy and transmitted that energy to the parent-body, somewhere in cosmic space.

Someday, having squeezed the planet dry, the Trisz would return to the void whence they came, or to other worlds still under their sway. When that happened, the last People would be left alone on Earth, to gasp out their sorry lives with their dying planet.

It was a grim picture, a picture etched into Kor Danay's mind by repeated lectures at the Institute. Further, the student Men had been conducted by the Masters to planets already deserted by the Trisz. There, they had viewed the withered bones of ancient worlds that had given up their life-blood to the remorseless siphoning of the Trisz. What had happened to the lost inhabitants of these worlds? Not even their bones remained on the wind-scoured plains in token of the living beings that once had swarmed there.

Perhaps it was already too late to save Earth . . . but the People might yet be saved. There were still young, green worlds in the galaxy. If the Trisz could be destroyed, their ships would remain to ferry Earth's People to far stars and more hospitable planets.

Kor Danay walked slowly through the city streets. The lower levels of Ka-si swarmed like a hill of desert ants. The city was the dwelling-place of Triszmen. Outlanders might visit, but not settle permanently, in the city, unless taken into the service of the Trisz.

Every comfort was built into the lavish apartments, every convenience in the colorful shops and amusement resorts. The People who worked for and with the Trisz were the favored of Earth. They wore elegantly styled, flamboyant costumes of fine materials under their yellow robes. Their living quarters had plumbing, automatic food preparers, artificial lighting, refrigeration, television, air-conditioning—all the comforts of a civilized race.

Sparkling signs lit up the canyoned streets with an interfluctuation of garish color. Huge televisor screens glared with outdoor public entertainment, news, tidbits of fancy to catch the attenton and absorb the interest. Ka-si was like a human city might be, if it had not been populated also by the Trisz. Humanity lived only on the lower levels. The work of the Triszmen was conducted on levels higher up, while above those, only the Trisz knew what took place. Up there, far above the gay, bright lights, the Trisz reigned alone, unapproachable, inexorable, invisible.

Kor had no hope of obtaining audience with the Trisz this evening, but he took himself to the Administration Center in search of possible information. A uniformed guard gave him the news he was looking for.

"Sorry, Sir. Audience with the Trisz takes place at half of the morning. You will have to come back then."

Though a Triszman, the guard had respect for the scarlet of Kor's office.

"Is there lodging to be had nearby, soldier?"

Kor drifted away with brief directions in mind. He joined the throng of people crowding the walk. Shortly, he noticed that a clear space was left around him as he walked, the crowd automatically parting to permit him untrammeled passage. The Scarlet Sages were respected both by the People and the Triszmen . . . even feared in a superstitious way. Occasionally, a passer-by knelt quickly and touched the hem of Kor's robe.

Kor repeated a philosophic beatitude on each occasion, but his mind was not on his surroundings. He had begun to extrapolate, seeking to find a clear course for his future actions. He could make nothing clear of the future—merely a muddled impression of encroaching menace.

The lodging to which the guard had directed him was a spire that thrust a half-mile into the evening sky. It must, he thought, pierce a half-mile as well into the rocky bed underlying the plain.

The entrance was gay with glittering glass and colorful plastic, a dazzling display of ever-changing hues that invited and repelled him at once. A stream of people went in and out through revolving doors which emitted puffs of cool breath from the air-conditioned interior. As Kor tarried, trying to make up his mind to enter, the feeling of menace which haunted him strengthened perceptibly.

He stood aside from the flow of human traffic, his mind locked in third-order rationalization of the situation. A type of logic that was not logic, his method of reasoning based its processes on dissimilarities rather than similarities, proceeded swiftly onward to conclusions completely divorced from the premises. The conscious mind being incapable of this dissimilar analysis, the function was carried on by the superconsciousness, called the "primary mind" in the vocabulary of the Men.

The Sages received intensive training in the development and use of this rational function, present in all human beings but submerged by the conscious attributes of the individual and generally referred to as "instinct" or "intuition." It was the Sages' recognition, isolation, and refinement of this function, as a non-logical method of rational apprehension, that made possible their complete control of mind and environment and produced that superbly knit thinking machine called a Man.

His reasoning told Kor that his life would be in immediate danger if he entered this building. Obviously, then, the guard who had directed him to this place had been under orders to do so. But if he did *not* enter the building, he was in even more positive danger. Wherein lay the difference between the two evils? His mind came up with the conclusion that his best action was to remain where he was. Another factor was about to enter the picture.

He waited, apparently amusing himself by watching the crowds go by. There was music on the air from radionic speakers spaced along the street. Across the street, a gigantic television screen flickered in full color its messages of entertainment, news, or whatever was being broadcast at the moment, synchronized with the noise made by the speakers.

It seemed to him that he could almost feel the eyes of the Trisz upon him, if it could be said that the Trisz possessed eyes. But, then, they did, of course—this horde of People represented the eyes of the Trisz, and the ears and hands as well; the Triszmen served their masters well.

A swirl of blue detached itself from the hurrying, colorful crowd and approached him. A Blue Brother, Kor observed. The man's visage was hawklike, deep-hued from desert sun, and saturnine.

"Sir!" The Blue Brother dipped his head before the Sage, in the salute to rank.

Kor returned the greeting with a similar nod. "Tranquillity, Brother!"

"Tranquillity, Sir. It is unusual to meet one of our Sages in Ka-si. Where is your Chapter?"

"I am unassigned," Kor replied stiffly, introducing himself. "I came to receive assignment from the Trisz, but I am told that reception is at half of the morning. It is now the first of the evening, and I was considering where I might spend the night."

The Blue Brother's expression was crafty. "You must be he who will occupy the Chapter of No-ka-si, which was recently vacated. I am Pol Seran, Blue Brother of the second district Lodge in No-ka-si. However, since it is not customary for a Sage to enter his Chapter before assignment, the hospitality of my own Lodge is open to you, if you will spend the night with me. You surely are not registered here?" He gestured toward the gaudy entrance.

"Not yet, Brother, but I had wished to be close for my audience."

The Blue Brother shrugged and made a face. "A public resort, Sir! Come—it is but a short distance to my Lodge. Do you have baggage?"

Kor's bags were still at the carriage depot, at the edge of the city, a long walk from this central spot.

"Easily picked up tomorrow," said Brother Pol. "I myself will bring you back in the morning in time for the Trisz reception. Come. The evening is getting along, and the street at night is no place for our Sages."

Was there a tinge of mockery in the Blue Brother's final words? Kor would have liked to ask a few leading questions, but the sense of unease which gripped him warned silence.

Momentarily he extrapolated the sum of his experiences, and decided that he would be safer in the sanctuary offered than anywhere else. It was not surprising to him that the Blue Brother fitted in well with the situation. The Blue Brothers were trained in the essence of service to the Trisz and the orders of their mission. It had to be that way. Only the Men themselves could be permitted to know fully what was going on.

For an instant, Val Shan's parting words hung tantalizingly in Kor's mind—". . . *find out just how dangerous you can be to the Trisz—and still live!*"

He had noticed the small surface cars plying the street, but had not realized they were public transportation until the Blue Brother hailed one and they got in. The seat was soft, luxuriously upholstered—uncomfortable to one who was used to sterner ways of travel.

The car was a product of Trisz technology, a manifestation of the simulated benevolence of the Trisz to their servants. Only the people of the Trisz cities had use of them, as well as of the air cars which flew from city to city. Such technological luxuries were on a par with home comforts, television, entertainment, the resorts, the synthetic liquors served in well-kept bars—for these were the temporal rewards the Trisz paid their faithful servants for their devotion and loyalty.

On the surface, it seemed that the Trisz were friends of mankind.

He was careful to attempt no prying conversation as they rode northward to No-ka-si. Kor Danay knew enough to beware the Trisz bearing gifts; the car was a nest of spy devices.

He did not doubt at all that the Trisz had sent the Blue Brother after him. They wanted him under control until a means could be devised to draw his fangs.

The Sage was eagerly interested in No-ka-si. If the Blue Brother's surmise were correct, and Kor should be assigned to this Chapter, then his surroundings had an added significance for him. Much as he had learned of the social aspects of the People, it had been all from lectures and books. For the first time, he was seeing an aggregation of People that covered more territory than the meager confines of a village.

The human city of No-ka-si was located to the north of the main city, separated from it by a narrow arid belt marking the ancient course of the Miz-zon. Nowhere in the surrounding waste was a tree or a blade of grass. The macadamized highway was laid on a bed of sterile sand, and ended on the paved streets of the smaller town.

Here there were no blazing electric lights. The streets were dimly lit by an occasional lamp-post that contained an oil-burning light. Windows were yellow rectangles of oil-lamp or candle illumination.

The streets were paved with a rough-surfaced plastic. The low, domed houses were built of a plastic similar to that in the buildings of the city. Everywhere, even in small courtyards and entries, the ground was completely plastic-paved in order to hold down as much as possible the ever-present dust. There were few enough trees left on Earth, no lumber at all for purposes of construction, and few metals; hence the prevailing use of plastic for building, hard, strong, colorful, made from the ubiquitous sand.

Deep artesian wells furnished both cities with water—precious water that was husbanded and re-used as often as it could be passed through the purifying tanks.

This careful conservation of water made the natural production of vegetable food impossible except in outlying areas, where only rare rainfall made a species of farming possible, or where association of the land with a surface stream permitted irrigation. Mostly, however, the People ate synthetic foods, many of which were imported from distant worlds in the far-flung commercial system of the Trisz, with the addition of a few vegetables grown in the hydroponic gardens of the Trisz cities.

People were not numerous in the streets of No-ka-si, but Kor noticed that some were Triszmen; and there was a solid proportion wearing the simple garments that proclaimed them Outlanders. The Triszmen living here lived with their Outlander families who were not permitted dwelling room in the Trisz city. Becoming a Triszman was a matter of application and careful selection, so that in most families of No-ka-si only the bread earner was in the service of the masters. The town was under the rulership of the regional Lord, since the Trisz were not directly concerned with its administration. The local Lord, however, was held responsible for keeping the peace and administering civic affairs throughout his own region and had to conform in all ways to the overlordship of the Trisz.

The Sage learned these things from the talk of his blue-robed companion as they rode into the town. Getting out when the vehicle stopped by the dark bulk of a building, Brother Pol gestured back the way they had come. The lighted spires of Ka-si reared like beacons into the night sky, and as Kor looked at them, a trillion tiny sparkles of irridescent light began to wing and cluster into a semiopaque curtain before the view.

"A beautiful effect!" he remarked. "What causes it?"

"Sandstorm," Brother Pol replied. "The city is protected by anti-sand projectors. They send up a curtain of radiation around the entire city. As the sand is blown into it, it is disrupted, and none can get through. When the wind blows extremely hard, it is often a most compelling sight."

Kor had noticed that a chill wind was rising, and now he began to feel the sting of flying grit. It was obvious that the human city had no such protection.

Brother Pol conducted the Sage to the low dome dwelling beside the larger Lodge, which was cubical, plain-surfaced in the style of Lodges everywhere. A gilded simulacrum of the Sun guarded the entrance to the Teacher's quarters, and broad, shallow steps led down at once from the entrance toward the sunken center of the dwelling: the living room, from which other rooms, at higher levels approached by stairs, gave off.

The cold of night had not yet penetrated into the Brother's house, but it was not uncomfortably warm, even though no air-conditioning was permitted here. A sweet smell of incense picked at Kor's nostrils. From somewhere, he heard the soft playing of a stringed instrument. In a moment, he spied the musician—a handsome girl of the People, dark-haired and well-shaped, squatting on a mat across the room. She plucked fitfully at the strings of her instrument as they came in.

Her presence made the Sage feel ill at ease, though he knew it was customary and accepted.

The Brother spoke to the girl. "That will do, Seta." He turned and whispered to Kor, "In deference to you, Sir, I will send her home tonight." He spoke kindly to the girl. "You may return to your people tonight, Seta. Please stop by the kitchen on your way out and instruct the cook to prepare dinner for His Eminence, Sir Kor. And do hurry on your way; a sandstorm is springing up and it may get nasty out."

The girl rose lithely and dropped her instrument on the mat. Her complexion was clear, her features regular and only a shade less than beautiful. She did not leave at once, but came toward Kor, dropped to one knee and touched the hem of his scarlet robe, raised it to her lips.

"Your blessing, Sir!"

"Tranquillity, daughter," Kor murmured mechanically.

The girl backed slowly from the room. Brother Pol smiled with saturnine amusement. "Splendid creature, isn't she? But of little interest to a newly graduated Sage such as yourself, Sir Kor!"

"Of no interest whatever," he replied distantly, then mentally kicked himself for having answered at all.

Brother Pol shrugged, still smiling.

## 6.  THE TRISZ

The audience hall of the Trisz was a large chamber, high up in the Administration Center, above the common levels of human occupation. The elevator had shot upward like a bullet for many second before slowing to a stop. Clusters of

People stood about the polished floor. Some were Outlanders and others wore colorful garb reserved for the Triszmen. Uniformed guards passed among them, alert to keep order. It was not quite the hour of half-morning.

Kor asked, "Must all these People take their turn in audience before the Trisz?"

Brother Pol made an expansive gesture around the perimeter of the audience chamber. Rich draperies shot scintillant reflections as they stirred gently in the air-conditioned breeze.

"Many more could be accommodated simultaneously. When the word is given, all go behind these draperies and are interviewed by the Trisz in smaller chambers. It gives the individual privacy."

"Each has audience before a separate Trisz, then?"

The Blue Brother shrugged and smiled. "Or the same Trisz. Is there any difference, as far as the Trisz are concerned? They seem to have the faculty of omnipresence."

Such a statement did not become a Blue Brother, but Kor Danay refrained from comment. Brother Pol had been trained to believe in the benevolence of the Trisz. "Which chamber ought I choose, Brother Pol?"

"It doesn't matter. Take the nearest. Everybody else will do the same."

"Are they all here for assignment somewhere, these People?"

"It does not always follow, Sir Kor, that audience means assignment. The Trisz are a gentle and benevolent race. They hear and act upon problems of the People, in addition to doing business with them."

"What kind of problems, Brother?"

"No problem is too small to deserve the attention and best effort of the Trisz," Brother Pol replied sanctimoniously. "A person may desire the love or companionship of one of the opposite sex. Or perhaps he is ambitious, and wants a position in the court of a lord, or in a business establishment, or in the service of the Trisz. Whatever it is, the Trisz, when properly petitioned, bend every effort to solve that problem to the individual's satisfaction."

Kor pondered the other's statements. "Do you mean to say that if a man wants a certain woman, the Trisz would forcibly procure her for him?"

"Forcibly? Oh, no, Sir! She would be procured—but not forcibly. Besides, the Trisz make it pleasant for her."

Advanced hypnosis, of course, the Sage remembered.

Where a problem could not be solved, or not solved to the petitioner's satisfaction, the same method of hypnosis made it seem to him that it had been. The textbooks had been specific on this point.

Brother Pol touched Kor's arm. "It's just about time, Sir. Let me remind you: when you speak to the Trisz, remember to use the customary language gestures. These are not only a sign of respect, as you have been taught, but also for recording by machines. The Trisz keep records for future generations, when your recorded voice may be unintelligible in the light of the language then spoken. The sign language will remain the same forever. As for the Trisz themselves, they need neither your voice nor the signs, as they read your discourse from your mind."

*Liar,* thought the Sage. Then he reconsidered. After all, Brother Pol knew no better. Everybody thought the Trisz could read minds, but the Sages knew otherwise. The respectful "gestures for the recorders," which law and custom commanded to be used in speaking to the Trisz, were a complex sign language which rapidly carried the speaker's meaning to the aliens. Kor Danay knew he could think anything he pleased in the presence of the Trisz, so long as his expression or attitude did not betray him.

A gong sounded a silvery note. A soft voice, borne on amplifiers, rustled across the tremendous audience chamber.

"Audience call . . . audience call. Approach the Trisz with humility, reverence, and sobriety. Gesture your prayers, and they will be answered. Audience call. Enter now into the presence of the Trisz!"

An excited stir passed through the crowd. Feet scraped on the gleaming floor. Garments swirled with color. Kor stepped to the nearest drapery and drew it back.

The room on the other side was small, not more than double a man's length on each side. Directly across from the entrance, the wall receded into a shallow bay or niche. The walls were bare. The floor was of the same gleaming plastic as in the audience hall.

He extrapolated briefly. He could detect nothing immediate save the usual feeling of menace. All the factors were still not present, he thought.

A column of pale, lovely fire stood suddenly in the niche . . . the Trisz. Kor realized he was not actually seeing the Trisz, which was an invisible manifestation of strange energy. Its presence was detectable only by its effect upon the air within the niche, and this effect was heightened by hidden projectors which sprayed the disturbed air molecules with changing hues of light. It was effective, Kor admitted, even as good as some of the stunts the Sages occasionally conjured in the Lodges to impress the People with the wonder-working.

He knelt on one knee and watched the Trisz fade through lavender, into pale green, retire into yellow, and emerge into glowing crimson.

Thin, tinny, and strident, the thought-impression that was the "voice" of the Trisz was impressed upon the Sage's conscious mind. "Hail, Man! The Trisz welcome you to Ka-si."

Kor made proper gestures of salutation, accompanying the signs with words intended for the audio-recorders . . . and for the ears of listening Triszmen, he had no doubt.

"Greetings in the name of Tranquillity, O mighty Trisz!"

The Trisz turned a tender pink. "I have looked into your mind, O Man. I perceive that you are Kor Danay, graduate Man of the Institute of Denver."

*Liar*, Kor thought. His registration papers had been sent ahead of him. "True, O mighty Trisz."

"The Trisz hold the Men in high esteem. They are ever in dear remembrance. The Trisz are the protector of the People—the Men are the weapon in the Trisz right hand."

"True, O Mighty Trisz," Kor acquiesced.

*What a farce,* he thought to himself. *Let's get the formalities over with. Go ahead, read my mind! You could detect my expanded superconsciousness, but my conscious mind is a closed book to you.*

The Trisz continued. "We are pleased with the thoughts of respect that flow from your mind, O Man. Your journey has been a long one, and difficult. You desire rest and tranquillity. But first, tell us of your journey."

Kor thought, *You want me to deny what happened, don't you? Then you'll claim to read the incidents from my mind and arrest me for attempting to restrain the truth. Well, I'll tell you what happened.*

He cast his glance upward.

"I owe my presence here only to the most happy fortune, so eventful was my journey!"

"Most interesting," squeaked the Trisz. "I read the details of your adventures in your thoughts, but please gesture the occurrence for the visual recorders."

Kor gestured his story with pious overtones. The Trisz

was uninterested in the first episode, where the Sage related that he had been attacked by "robbers" disguised in the garb of loyal servants of the Trisz; but its interest revived with the account of the incident at the inn—described from the Sage's point of view.

Suspicion, prime virtue of the conqueror, held the Trisz in thrall. It put questions apparently designed to lead the Sage into some kind of semantic trap, but Kor evaded with a liberal use of platitudes.

"This has been very interesting for the records," the Trisz said. There was a moment of thoughtful pause, then the Trisz went on, "Your registration has been received and approved, Man, for assignment to the Chapter of No-ka-si. I discern from your thoughts that you passed last night in the quarters of Blue Brother Pol, who awaits you now in the central audience chamber. The floor guard has been instructed to deliver to him your orders of assignment. He will conduct you to your new post in the Lodge of the No-ka-si region and perform the proper introductions. You will deliver yourself now into his guidance. Good luck attend you, Man."

"Tranquillity, O mighty Trisz!"

Kor rose and went backward out of the chamber.

# 7.   LADY SOMA

Blue Brother Set Horan folded his pudgy hands, his demeanor enhanced by a cherubic smile that played across his round features.

"My dear," said he, with a tone of finality, "it has to be that way, don't you see? However far the game must be played, it simply has got to be played as we are playing it. There are no ifs, ands, or buts about it."

The young woman seated opposite him bit her full underlip. She was lovely, a woman of the desert People. Her hair was a deep chestnut, arranged about her face in the popular style then fashionable among the well to do. She set firm red lips and glared at the Blue Brother with eyes of deep sea-green.

"I tell you it is a dangerous game we are playing, Brother Set. Suppose something should go wrong? You know what Val Shan has said."

Brother Set's amiable features lost none of their look of cherubic cheer. "Certainly it's dangerous, but he has gotten this far, hasn't he? You know as well as I that a Sage has to live dangerously—even this one. Val Shan is of the opinion that our lad is of particular importance to the plans of the Men. Well, that remains to be seen. I'm working under double orders, you know."

"You mean—"

"Of course! According to Val Shan's thinking, we must lose no more time than necessary in getting this particular Man to the Organization. And I have orders from the Trisz, relayed through the City Council of Triszmen, to lose no time saddling him with a charge that will merit a public execution. Do you think it has been easy for me, Lady Soma?"

The Lady Soma held a handkerchief against her lips. "That is what I mean about its being dangerous. We both run a grave risk of being killed—if not by the Trisz, then by *him*."

Brother Set toyed a moment with a stylus, tapping the blunt end against his teeth, his expression thoughtful. "Well," he sighed at last, putting the stylus down, "it would be no more than I expected when I first undertook this hide-and-seek game years ago." He smiled. "Though I will say, my dear Lady Soma, that you are entirely too lovely and young to die!"

"Thank you," she replied coolly. "At least, you have given me the well-known skin of the teeth to escape by!"

"Then be thankful for that much," chuckled the rotund Blue Brother. "But you neglect to take our Sage himself into consideration." He sighed and shook his head sadly. "I wish I had the brains—or whatever it takes—to be chosen for Manhood! As it is—well, I have been fortunate, my dear. You see me now, a teacher of the Blue Order, raised to the honor of doing a job worthy of a Man"—he grimaced—"without the satisfaction of knowing, when I die, that I could have smeared the lot of them if it weren't for my confounded Oath!"

"Brother Set!"

"Ho! I know—envy does not become a Brother. But just the same, my dear, I know a few of the things a Man can do, and if I had their powers at my disposal, I'd do a little house cleaning of my own!" He chuckled shortly. "The Masters most likely took cognizance of this temperamental attitude of mine, which explains why I was relegated to this." He shook the hem of his blue robe.

"I'm proud, though, to be able to help the Men. But it worries me, this playing both ends against the middle—especially when *I'm* in the middle!"

The girl laid her hand softly upon his. "We are most fortunate you did *not* become a Sage, Brother Set! Who could have served half so well as you?"

He leaned back in his plastic chair, beaming with pleasure. "You say the nicest things, my dear!" He glanced at a chronometer on the wall and started up. "Good Lord! It's after half-morning! They'll be here any minute! Are you sure now that you have everything in mind? We can't slip up on this, or—" He passed a rigid forefinger significantly across his throat.

"If I only knew *how* he could get out of it!"

"I told you about the first two attempts that were made on his life. Remember what he did to those two Triszman Thugs? He picked one up and threw him at the other! Ho, ho! The woman told us about that; the men wouldn't! And that murderer-for-hire—know where he is now? Out exhorting uprightness on street corners! Resourceful, our Man! Lives up to the highest tradition of his Sagecraft—and you can't say I didn't know he would!"

The Lady Soma patted his hand again. "I know. You wouldn't have sent those men against him to be killed. You knew he'd spare them."

"That's what I mean about being a Man," Brother Set interjected. "For all I'm supposed to be a teacher, I've got something of the ruffian in me, too. I'd have torn 'em apart!"

"Silly!" Soma laughed with clear, tinkling merriment. "You'd have done nothing of the kind!"

Brother Set grinned and winked. "And now maybe you feel better about the plan, eh?"

She started to frown, then smiled quickly at his droll expression. "I guess I am mostly thinking of it from my own viewpoint." She shuddered. "I'd hate to have anybody put *me* in that position."

"Nobody shall. Now pull yourself together. I think I hear them coming."

A tutor, newly graduated into the ranks of Blue Brotherhood, preceded Kor and Brother Pol into the room.

Kor Danay paused on the threshold, suddenly alert.

Brother Set's round features and saintly smile matched perfectly the image purloined from the mind of the assassin. Kor's second impression as he advanced warily into the room was a startled one of sheer loveliness as he caught sight of Lady Soma.

Brother Pol quickly made introduction between the Blue Brother Set and Kor in accordance with protocol. This was carried over by Brother Set to include Lady Soma.

"—daughter of Lord Roen Gol, esteemed resident Lord of our own Ka-si district, civil functionary, protector of the People, etc., etc. You know what I mean?"

The ice was quite thoroughly broken from the beginning. Kor took special delight in the conversation that followed the departure of Brother Pol, in which Lady Soma was an interested participant.

She finally took her leave, and the Sage found himself alone with the Blue Brother whom he had cause to distrust most heartily.

Now that he was settled in the quarters occupied by his predecessor, a certain Sir Ten Roga, Kor Danay had set this conference with Brother Set to discuss the affairs of the Chapter. While he was much concerned to learn what had happened to Sir Ten, he felt that he had reason not to let this concern become too apparent.

He found many things to surprise him—for one, the population of the Ka-si region. He had not thought the desert would support so many. Brother Set began to explain matters of service personnel, who were drawn from the desert dwellers.

"The Civil Service examinations are constantly open, calling for volunteers to become Triszmen in one capacity or another. We have a rather heavy drain on volunteers from this region. Since few are required in Ka-si itself, many are sent to other parts of the world, as need requires. Some, of course, are called for training as spacemen to man the Trisz vessels. And then, of course, there are the colonies."

"The colonies, Brother?"

"You have not heard of the colonies, Sir? According to information, there are many worlds throughout the galaxy, each capable of supporting a large population. These worlds are populated only slightly, or not at all. The Trisz, therefore, are introducing Earth People to these foreign

41

worlds—colonizing them, as it were, for the better future of mankind and the galaxy as a whole. The Trisz are a kind and benevolent race, Sir."

"Yes—yes, of course," Kor interposed. He remembered now a lecture on this subject at the Institute. What had been the point? Certain of the People were selected from time to time for these colonizing ventures, and whisked mysteriously off into space. In their desire to attain a future liaison with these colonized worlds of People, the Men had attempted to discover where they had been taken, but the search so far had not met with success.

He hazarded a question. "Are the colonists sent to any particular System in this or any other particular galaxy?"

"Who knows where they go, Sir Kor? That is the business of the benevolent Trisz, who seek always the welfare of the People. Getting to the point, Sir, we are furnishing a quota of five hundred colonists very soon. Only a few more volunteers need to be signed up."

"What happens if you fall short in your quota?"

Brother Set raised startled eyebrows, as if the question were unheard of. "Sir, we *never* fall short!"

"I see." Kor ground his teeth together and wished mightily he dared probe just once behind that saintly mask. "Brother Set, what happened to the Sage whose Chapter I am taking over?"

Brother Set looked sad. He did feel genuinely sad about it—Sir Ten had been a regular fellow to work with—but he had to continue playing with the young man across from him.

"Sir Ten Roga loved to ride horseback on the desert. He went one day alone—and vanished."

That was possible, Kor thought, but not probable. Being a Man, Sir Ten could easily have vanished off the face of the Earth; but also, being a Man, he could not have done so without permission of the Institute . . . and the Institute would never have permitted it.

"Did you not find his body, Brother?"

"Yes—that is, I *think* we did. We found his horse's body, and a few fragments of our Sage's robe and buskins. The horse had stumbled in a hole and broken its leg. Obviously, Sir Ten was thrown and either killed outright, or injured and made easy prey for the desert wolves."

Kor was satisfied. Now he knew that Brother Set was a liar. No living thing could kill a Man in any way whatsoever without his consent. Sir Ten would instantaneously have compensated for such a fall and been unharmed.

"The Trisz murdered Sir Ten!"

Brother Set pursed his lips, shrugged his shoulders and spread his hands expressively.

It was desired that Kor Danay should think so. The Lady Soma thought so also. Only Brother Set knew that Sir Ten had been recalled to the Organization of Men—the underground branch of the Brotherhood—especially to make a place for Kor Danay in this particular Chapter.

Kor's first Lodge day in his new post made him nervous. There was so much to do, so much to attend to. In spite of his training, he was new to it all. Tutors flew hither and yon in response to Brother Set's directions. The Sage paced his study, preparing himself for his planned address.

A mumbling uproar from outside percolated through the train of his thought and roughened the edge of the fine prose he was constructing. He threw back his shoulders in annoyance and went swiftly into the outer Lodge in search of the Blue Brother.

"Are the People gathering already for the meeting? It still lacks an hour."

The Brother beamed his saintly smile. "Some idiot out there is making a fuss about having seen the light. He has quite a crowd around him, exhorting from the Lodge steps."

"I should like to hear him," Kor said. "It is possible, Brother, that we might learn something from the simple exhortation of the People."

"I doubt it," Brother Set muttered.

Kor went to the Lodge door and opened it a crack. A small, shabbily dressed Person stood on the steps a few feet below him, exhorting a sizable crowd of laborers, merchants, housewives, Triszmen, and a few girls. The man's voice was high-pitched, filled with fervor and ecstasy.

"—and I would not be here now," he cried, "if I had not seen with my own eyes the glory of which I speak! No! But as I entered that room, a criminal, awareness came unto me, and . . ."

The crowd rumbled.

"Proof, fellow! Give us proof!"

"You ask for proof! Very well. I will give you the proof He gave unto me!"

There was a moment of breath-catching silence. The man on the steps drew himself erect. It was a stirring sight. Every eye centered on that slight figure above the crowd, every mind attuned to the mystery of enlightenment.

As the silence prolonged itself into a hush, the speaker slowly raised clasped hands over his head, and Kor started. Into the astounded eyes of the crowd lanced a brilliant gleam of brightly raying luminescence.

"Putting on a show, is he?" Brother Set asked at the Sage's elbow.

Kor gestured to the crack of the door. "See for yourself."

Brother Set looked. "Well, well. Very interesting!"

"Do you think it a genuine miracle?" Kor asked, making a great effort toward restraining a smile.

Brother Set smiled openly and disarmingly. "Frankly, no." He cast Kor one of his droll looks. "Do you?"

As the Sage hesitated, he added, "You needn't answer that, Sir!"

## 8.  AMBUSH

Kor's attempt to extrapolate forthcoming events was a dismal failure. Ordinarily, he should have been able to procure a pretty clear picture of events for a period a full day ahead. Beyond that, he should have been able to make a rational prediction with a reasonable certitude of exactness.

Instead, the reward of his effort was simply a continued feeling of unease, an apprehension, on the non-verbal level, of menace.

About midmorning, a letter came for Kor Danay, delivered by a lackey from the staff of Lord Roen Gol, routed through Brother Set, and presented upon a silver salver by a blue-robed acolyte.

Kor Danay broke the seal, unfolded the paper, and scanned the message with pleasure, noting the neat, feminine script, followed by the signature of Lady Soma Gol. He read it again, not because his glance had missed anything, but to let his eyes linger upon this token of her hand. The loops and whorls of her writing acted as a tonic to his feelings, and the Sage glowed with a new sense of well-being.

He tried to appear casual as he strolled out and accosted

Brother Set. "I have just received some sort of an invitation —from the young lady who was here the other day. What's her name?"

Brother Set arched his eyebrows. "It is an odd thing for a Sage to have a faulty memory, Sir. You doubtless refer to the Lady Soma, daughter of Lord Roen Gol . . ."

Kor snapped his fingers. "Yes—yes! Lady Soma. This invitation, it appears, is to some kind of formal reception. Don't you think it will be a boring sort of affair?"

The Blue Brother frowned and wagged his head. "On the contrary, Sir! It is customary for the district lord to receive the new Man into his Chapter, and distinctly an honor."

The rotund teacher donned his most cherubic smile, but Kor noticed that there was no humor about his eyes. He thought, *This could be a trap.* A mental picture of the Lady Soma swam in his mind, and he shook his head. "Perhaps I had better go."

"I rather guess you had! You wouldn't want to anger our local lord, would you? Not to mention his lovely daughter!"

"The invitation is from the Lady Soma, not Lord Roen Gol."

"So the Lady Soma is her father's secretary. What is strange about that? Naturally, she takes care of the details of her father's social affairs. And it will be an affair, you can count on that."

"Very well. I will go."

"Of course. Arrangements have already been made."

"You mean to say you read that note before I did?"

"Certainly. A letter of acceptance has already been dispatched to her ladyship."

"The letter was sealed," Kor pressed stubbornly, feeling a slow rise of anger.

"So it was sealed! I can unseal and seal a letter. Officially, I am your secretary, and it is my duty—"

"Enough!" Kor snapped. "Do you forget who I am?"

"Pardon, your Serenity," apologized Brother Set, injecting a tone of irony into the seldon-used title. "We will touch upon the matter later. Right now, we must concern ourselves with the matter of the five hundred colonists. They are embarking today, and you and I will have to be on hand at the spaceport this afternoon to take care of a few last minute matters."

"What kind of matters?"

"For one, you will speak to the colonists."

"What am I supposed to say?"

"The usual things. Bon voyage—carry on the traditions of Earth. The usual rigmarole."

Kor said coldly, "I don't think I like the ill-concealed levity with which you treat matters of this nature, Brother Set!"

While Kor busied himself over an address to be delivered to the departing colonists, Brother Set took advantage of the Sage's absorption to mount a carriage and make a hasty trip to the residence of Lord Roen Gol, where he closeted himself with his Lordship and the Lady Soma. At the conclusion of their brief interview, the three shook hands solemnly.

"Neither of you will have a moment to lose," the Blue Brother warned. "Lord Roen, sir, are you sure all is in readiness?"

Lord Roen, a tall, bluff man with iron-gray hair and piercing eyes, nodded shortly. "The fastest horses in my stable have been made ready, Brother. When the time comes, I shall act without a moment's hesitation."

"You realize that it means losing everything?"

Lord Roen Gol shrugged, and a slight smile tinged his stern lips. "What is it to lose everything—when everything is as nothing compared to the greater goal?" He stroked his daughter's hair fondly. "So long as I do not lose my dearest possession . . ."

The Lady Soma smiled quickly up at him, green eyes a-light. "You know I can take care of myself, Father! And I will see you again—afterward."

Brother Set laid a finger against his lips. "Tut! Let us not dwell on the unpleasant aspects. Now, I must hurry back and whip my boy some more."

The Blue Brother chuckled at Soma's suddenly startled look. "Must keep him on the *qui vive,* you know. It would never do to let him become complacent. My whip, of course, is only metaphorical, but I have been laying it on heavily."

He looked momentarily unhappy. "Perhaps too heavily —but no. It is essential that he thoroughly dislike and mistrust me. He must depend entirely on himself. Well, to-night's the affair, and I can keep him busy this afternoon. After that, it's up to you two—we may not meet again."

He turned suddenly and put his back to them. His voice came muffled over his shoulder. "Maybe I'll get used to carrying on alone, but I doubt it."

The Trisz spaceport was located within the tallest and broadest of the buildings within the city. From their cradles deep within the monstrous edifice, the magnetically operated spaceships of the Trisz took off for far worlds; and as quickly as they were gone, the cradles received those coming in from the deeps of space.

Mostly, these were supply vessels that kept linked the worlds under the domination of the Trisz. A little space travel was permitted, but not enough to constitute a tourist condition. Men of business and trade occasionally traveled to other worlds; and rarely, extra-terrestrials arrived at one city or another on Earth to observe methods, look after legal or financial interests, and so forth. Mass travel was prohibited.

Kor Danay had amused himself watching the ovoid vessels rise from the spaceport and waft gently upward toward the stratosphere. Once in space, of course, the vessels lanced into light-year-devouring overdrive; but at top speed, their pace was a crawl compared to the almost instantaneous maneuverability of the Men.

He had wanted to observe these vessels close at hand, and was disappointed to find that he must speak to the colonists many floors below the spaceport levels. As the Sage spoke, his voice was carried to the farthest reaches of the hall by spaced amplifiers.

He searched the crowd casually, wondering what type of People these were who willingly abandoned their homes and their world to embark into the unknown. Mostly, they were rough Outlanders, shabbily dressed and ill fed. The crowd was about evenly divided between the sexes, and not all of the women were young. Apparently, age did not constitute a matter of preference.

A blinding ball of light waxed in a far corner of the hall as the Sage concluded the formalities. He got down quickly from the speaking platform and sought out Brother Set, who was talking over lading details with a section of the Triszman guard.

"You remember the convert with the glowing hands, Brother? He is in this Crowd."

Brother Set smiled angelically. "Indeed, Sir?"

"It is strange . . ." Kor began.

"What is strange about it? There is room in the colonies for the upright, as well as the unregenerate."

Kor hesitated and bit his lip. He recalled the interest the Trisz had taken in the man with the glowing hands. Had the

47

fellow willingly volunteered for this mission? Or had other methods been resorted to? Kor could guess that the man's presence had made the Trisz nervous . . .

"Shall we go?" Brother Set murmured beside him. "There are so many here—and so few of them wash."

He decided to walk to Lord Roen Gol's reception that evening. Kor told himself that this was the safest course.

Brother Set protested this arrangement.

"I can take care of myself," the Sage observed pointedly.

Brother Set shrugged and sighed. "It is not propriety, Sir, that our Sages gallivant the streets alone by night. Which route do you take?"

"As I am a Man, my way is my own. Good evening, Brother Set."

Lord Roen Gol's imposing residence lay at the northward edge of town, a distance of over a mile from the Scarlet Chapel. The Sun had barely set when Kor started out, and the western sky was a cauldron of seething scarlet, banded bright pink and streaming with green. Sand clouds high in the atmosphere were responsible for the colors, both by refraction and reflection. Mirages, too, were common in the desert air, and fantastic lights were often seen to play far up above the surface for the space of an hour or so after sunset.

Kor Danay strode along, past lamplit windows and open doors that exhaled a breath of the day's heat, drawn out by the encroaching chill of night. The air was baited with cooking smells and the synthetic beer, vibrant with a continuous vociferation and clack of conversation.

It was amazing, he thought, in how short a time he had become accustomed to the sights and clamor of the world. His years at the Institute had faded into the background of his consciousness, and seemed now scarcely ever to have been. In those years, the People had been nothing to him save statistics in a book.

Now he had seen the People at their everyday life, and it occurred to him that there was less difference than he had thought between the Men and the People. True, the Men were superior to the People. But no longer in the connotation he had formerly cherished. The Men were people of a different order, trained to bring out their latent capabilities, given direction and set upon a lasting purpose in life. The People simply existed, quarreling, fighting, loving, being gay and sad by turns, being completely human.

His way through the streets of No-ka-si debouched finally into a broad thoroughfare that was doubly lined with palms. Woody fronds rattled in the night breeze, seemed to crackle in the cold. The ground lost its heat quickly to the arid air, once the Sun had set, and nights always were cold on Earth.

The palm-lined avenue led straight to the crest of a low knoll, atop which glimmered Lord Roen Gol's sprawling residence.

Kor tested the bark of one of the palms with his thumbnail. The tree was real, all right. He wondered how much water was required to keep these trees alive, and if even a lord had the right to divert so much. By and by, he came upon flowers along the way, gorgeous blooms that had been bred to wrest a hardy livelihood from the grudging soil and to withstand the extremes of heat and cold normal in a single solar revolution.

Carriages went by as he strolled up the avenue. Obviously, Lord Roen's reception was to be a lavish affair. He entered finally the broad parking place before the official residence, picked his way among parked carriages and restive horses, until he came at last to the brightly lit doorway.

Lord Roen Gol was a tall man and heavily built, with high cheekbones and a jutting beak of a nose. His eyes, sea-green like those of his lovely daughter, held a piercing and inquisitive stare. He greeted Kor's arrival in person, quickly wrung his hand. "My pleasure, Sir!"

The Sage replied, "My gratitude, Lord!"

They linked arms on the way into the reception room where the guests milled in light, warmth, and shrill talkativeness. The air was heavy with the smell of perfumes; smoke from the scented cigars of the gentlemen drifted in billowing strata. Musical instruments caressed by a score of scantily clad girls issued a continuous, monotonous tinkle of gaiety.

Brightness and revelry were everywhere, but none of it meant anything at all to Kor Danay—until he met the Lady Soma again.

What had his memory of her been, he asked himself, that it seemed so shabby in the light of her real presence? Kor took her hand, his eyes caught and held by the compelling, sea-green charm of her gaze.

He spoke to the father, without taking his eyes from the daughter. "Your house is richly blessed, Lord."

Lord Roen chuckled genially, patted his daughter's arm. "Be wary of her, Sir Kor!"

The girl flashed her father a look which was not lost upon the Sage, and the lord sobered at once. He bowed shortly, excused himself, and left the two alone.

"His Lordship seems troubled about something," Kor began.

The girl shook her head quickly. "Not at all. It's a terrific strain playing host to all these people, and poor Daddy's been so overworked lately . . ."

He strolled with her through the enveloping crowd, her hand on his arm. She was quiet, walked with eyes cast down; it seemed, Kor thought, that she was embarrassed.

"Let me introduce you to the guests," she said suddenly, looking up into his face with a sudden reversal of expression, smiling, eyes sparkling. "They've all come to meet you, of course."

A sense of foreboding swirled over Kor. He should have extrapolated this encounter, he thought, but it was too late now to profit from it, even if he were successful at it. He turned the task over to his superconsciousness, with a silent command to deliver any warning of danger, and forgot his foreboding in the sensations of the moment.

It seemed hours before dinner was announced, and by then, Kor had met, formally, nearly all the more important guests. Each name and face was properly filed in his memory. He would be able at any future time to recognize, or recall by name and appearance, any whom he had met tonight—if he should live so long, he thought wryly.

The dinner was long and heavy. There were speeches. Kor himself had to stand and formally acknowledge introduction to the crowd in a body. At last, Lord Roen clapped his hands and the tables broke up. The guests drifted toward the next room, where music and dancing had begun already.

Kor got to his feet and offered his arm to Lady Soma. As they strolled into the ballroom, Soma almost clung to his arm; her weight dragged him down. He put his arm around her in alarm. "Soma . . . are you ill?"

She shook her head, then nodded. A look of misery swam in her eyes. "It—it's nothing. Let's—let's go out on the terrace."

"Of course!"

The air was warm and stuffy—too much for her, Kor thought. He turned obediently with her in the direction of wide doors that stood open upon the nighted expanse of a terrace. As he did so, a spear point of shrill menace darted from his superconsciousness. Death lurked on the terrace!

The Sage's eyes narrowed. Lady Soma seemed to be in agony. She couldn't be acting, he told himself. Her shoulders were bent, she held her head low and breathed with difficulty, as if she were sobbing.

He steered her quickly through the dancing throng, scorning the jangle of alarm bells in his mind.

The air on the terrace was bitingly cold. A great, golden moon, occupying a full eighth of the quadrant, stood high in the eastern sky. It hung there like a glowing orange shield, every crater, every ridge, rill, and ancient "sea" easily discernible to the naked eye. The moon hung close to Roche's limit. Had the oceans and seas of old still existed, the height of their tides would have staggered the imagination.

But the seas were only stagnant ponds; and someday relatively soon, the moon would approach closer until it would rend itself asunder in a mighty conflict of gravitational forces. But there would be none on Earth then to see the majesty of its destruction, or to suffer from its hurtling fragments. There would be nothing left save the bleached bones of a world bled dry by the Trisz.

But tonight in its near fullness, the moon cast an orange glow upon the garden and terrace of Lord Roen Gol, and Kor Danay felt himself transfixed again by the voiceless urging of his superconscious mind.

He held the girl close in his arms, wrapping a fold of his cloak around her.

"Soma! Are you ill?" he had asked this question once before. That he asked it again was indicative of the intensity of his desire that illness was all it might be. A Sage possessed powers in this direction also, and to cleanse her of illness would take him only a moment.

The Lady Soma shook herself free of his cloak, thrust his supporting arm aside, and walked unsteadily to the balustrade. She toyed with a cluster of blooms that dispelled their fragrance on the frigid night.

"Lovely, aren't they? Hydroponics, of course. The tanks are hidden in the stonework."

That could not be all she had brought him out here to say.

"Something is wrong," he protested. "I should like to know what it is."

She whirled suddenly, thrusting the cluster of flowers behind her. The touch of her hand upon his arm was like the alighting of a frantic bird.

Her cheeks were pale, her eyes dark and stormy. She drew red lips away from white, even teeth. "I brought you out here, Sir Kor—" She stopped, gathered her forces, and continued, "—to have you killed!"


## 9.   POWER OF A MAN

Kor stepped back a pace. Soma stood rigid against the balustrade.

"I do not kill easily!" he said.

His mind opened automatically, swept out like an expanding spring of tempered steel. He felt the impingement of inimical presences upon his consciousness. He counted them. One, two, three, four, five, six. Six featureless shapes lurked in the deep shadow of palms in Lord Roen Gol's garden.

Kor Danay sensed the infinitesmal stir of their bodily electrons. He reduced his vibratory rate of perception until he was merely conscious of the air whistling in and out of their lungs, the unconscious slipping of one muscle upon another, the stirring of the blood in their veins. One of the lurkers had an uneven heartbeat, he noted in passing; probably that one would not live long.

Kor straightened, shaking out his cloak so that it fell cleanly from his shoulders. "You supposed it would take six of your killers, Lady Soma? I perceive that many in your garden."

His tone dripped scorn, a scorn that hid the hurt and bewilderment that had left him stricken. How had he been wrong? Why had she done this? Was it not the machination of her father, that genial politican dancing in the next room with some fat, elderly dowager? Was not the Blue Brother also at fault, and beyond them all, the Trisz?

A burst of tinkling music followed by a wave of applause surged through the doors and stormed the terrace.

"No," she whispered. "Be quiet. There is time. I was not to have told you that, only to bring you here, put you at your ease, then go back inside for my wrap. I—I am trying to help you!"

"Which," Kor asked wonderingly, "is the real you?"

She stepped toward him. "Come, your arm, Sir Kor. Embrace me!"

"The embrace—of death?"

"Of life! You are safe so long as I am with you. But I cannot stay long."

Her manner belied her words, for she laughed excitedly as she talked. "Quickly! Your arm, Sir Kor!"

Slowly, the Sage obeyed. She squirmed quickly into his grasp. "Listen, closely. I know you can detect those men in the garden. Be ready to act if one of them moves, but pretend to be interested in me. Smile—if you can. Those men in the garden are Trisz Thugs. Do you know what Thugs are?"

Kor knew. They were the secret execution corps of the Trisz. He nodded, and smiled.

"In a few moments," Lady Soma continued breathlessly, "I must go back in and leave you here alone. The instant I am safely inside the door, the Thugs have their orders to blast you where you stand."

"Why are you telling me this?"

He kept his mind opened, alert for the least motion among the six. All stood motionelss, waiting.

"Why do you think?"

For a moment, an indescribable feeling of giddiness rushed over Kor. He thrust it aside. "I cannot believe you have a personal reason, Lady Soma."

She smiled as she looked up into his eyes, but her own were dark with the turmoil of her thoughts. "Perhaps; perhaps not. Let us say this, then—that I am a woman of the People. My father is lord of this region. Do we not also owe a duty to the People, even as great as that assumed by the Men?"

Kor was troubled. What did she know of the Men's duty toward the People?

She said, "Sir Ten Roga was a great friend, Kor. We know things, my father and I, that we cannot tell even to you—and we know things about the Men that neither the People nor the Trisz know. Is that enough? Must I tell you also that not only is your own life forfeit, but that of my father, also?" She paused to control the rising passion in her voice.

"Let me tell it to you quickly. I must not linger too long. You see me now as the daughter of my father. I am also a spy in the city. I work on the staff of the Trisz Extrapolator. My father does not know that, of course. He would object if he did. But he has been playing a dangerous game, himself. He is allied with the Men, Kor. To help drive the Trisz out of our world!"

The Sage listened calmly, analyzing the words that fell from her lips. The semantics were clean and proper; he detected no overtones of falsehood. "Go on," he said quietly.

"Recently my father concluded a brotherhood pact with the Lord of Set-loo. Before, there had been some feuding between them, and flare-ups of fighting between our opposing troops were common. The Lord of Set-loo misunderstood certain things, but my father ironed out these difficulties with him. The Trisz were at the bottom of the discord, of course. It is an open secret that they encourage poor relations among the various districts. My father undertook to make his pact with the Lord of Set-loo in secret, but the Trisz found out. The Trisz punish secrecy of this kind with death. Your death will be the signal for my father's arrest. He will be publicly executed for your murder."

"Not all you say is understandable."

"I cannot make it plainer. There is not time. My real identity is not known where I serve the Trisz. I was chosen to attend this function as my other self, to lure you within range of the Thugs. I had to let myself be chosen, you see, because only I could have given you warning!"

She moved away from him. "Now there is no more time. I must go in and get my wrap."

"Wait!" Kor caught her by the shoulder, spun her around to face him. "You would walk off like this, knowing that in another moment I will be blasted to a charred crust?"

She smiled, calmly possessed of herself. "Not you, Kor. I told you I know things about the Men. You can save yourself. I have given you the opportunity. Goodbye, Kor."

"Wait!" She hesitated, poised. He rushed on. "If you are asked ever to identify me—swear you have never seen me before. Claim that you talked with an impostor here tonight. You understand?"

She nodded, wide-eyed, then hurried through the open doors.

And Kor Danay reacted. The softly swaying palm fronds froze into icy petals. All sound stopped. The air was solid around him. The universe stood still.

The action he must follow came to him in a burst of rationalization. With infinite deliberation, he palped with his mind the six motionless figures in the garden. There was one about his own size.

The time-stasis—actually, the acceleration of the Sage's consciousness of time—brought its own peculiar set of conditions into play. Kor was living at an extremely high rate of molecular vibration. Every molecule in his body vibrated at such tremendous speed that his body no longer bore any relationship to normal matter, but was matter beyond matter. If he continued to remain in one position long enough for an observer's eye to react, he would seem to have disappeared completely. What he had to do required doing in that brief fraction of a second before he would appear to vanish into nothing before the eyes of the watching Thugs.

Kor's body vibrated at a vastly accelerated time rate, and his mind with it, but the air around him was not affected. It held him as if in a strait jacket until he expanded the influence of the time-stasis to include a small space around him. Then he sighted a straight path to the Thug he had chosen for reason of his size, and cast a pathway of accelerated air molecules ahead of him as he went.

The Thug lay on the ground, frozen, immobile, squinting along the barrel of an ugly-looking energy weapon. *Already,* Kor thought, *his finger is tightening on the release stud.*

The Thug's body seemed hard as a rock. Kor could not have budged him had he tried. The matter now composing the Sage's body could have no effect upon matter of the world he had left. Except for the supersensitive apperception of his mind, Kor would have been blind in this lightless, soundless universe of his own.

Mentally, he adjusted the influence of the time-stasis to include the Thug, bringing them together into the same vibratory rate, and kicked him hard on the jaw before he could stir. The Thug grunted and collapsed.

Quickly, Kor stripped himself of his scarlet garments and changed clothing with the unconscious Thug. That done, he slung the fellow over his shoulder, ran with him back to the terrace, and stood him in exactly the spot that the Sage himself had occupied before, restoring the Thug to consciousness and withdrawing the influence of the time-stasis as he did so.

The Thug stood like a statue in the rigid garments of the Sage. Kor ran back to the Thug's deserted post, picked up the discarded weapon, and returned his time rate to normal.

The Thug stood where Kor Danay had left him. He had started to lift his arms, and in a moment he would have shouted. The Lady Soma's back flashed out of sight into the maelstrom of dancers within the ballroom.

The fractional second was past. None could have seen the substitution. Five lances of flame rayed out of the darkness—and an instant behind, a sixth, as the Sage brought his captured weapon into play. The gesticulating figure on the terrace writhed in coruscating flame, vanished behind the flower-covered balustrade. The hideous noise of the energy weapons stuttered into silence.

*Very well,* Kor thought grimly. *Let us see what comes now.*

He ran after the sound of racing footsteps as the Thugs sped for the open. He almost collided with the group as they reached the first row of town houses. One, who seemed to be the leader, was haranguing the rest; he stopped as Kor came running up.

"There you are, Aln! You were slow. Get this: we scatter here and work back toward the city from different directions to avoid suspicion. You all know why we cannot be connected with this business. Now, get going!"

The Thugs darted off in all directions. The Sage dallied a moment, then strolled leisurely away, his weapon hidden under the rough brown cloak he had taken from the late Aln.

He could imagine the commotion at the palace of Lord Roen Gol. He thought of the Lady Soma, and a warmth enfolded him. He hoped she would not think the smoking wreck on her father's terrace was Kor Danay. He paused, let his mind flash back and touch that corpse. Swirling electrons flashed through the Sage's consciousness, a flood of bright stars that swarmed down as if to engulf him. His mind was in the body of the dead man, sorting, classifying, photographing the structure of its matter down to the last element. He would need the matrix to complete the plan which had come to him.

Kor knew what he had to do, if he wanted to return to his Lodge. And return he must, if he would get to the bottom of this business. But that was not the whole reason, either; part of it was contained in a pair of sparkling, sea-green eyes, and in warm, enfolding arms.

He swept his surroundings with his expanding mind,

seeking an empty dwelling. The hour was late, and in the pallid moonglow, the city slept. The moon rode above the city like a gargantuan, pock-marked face, featureless and cold.

Somewhere, there must be an empty house. He sensed it from a distance, reconnoitered its surroundings. No living soul was abroad. The house was unfurnished and empty.

He selected a spot in the central living chamber. His mind sought a pattern of electrons in the smooth plastic floor. The Sage made the change-over without a pause in his stride and came to a halt in the middle of the deserted living room.

He squatted on the hard floor. In the back of his mind electrons swirled, coalesced, drove in a quickening stream and hovered in the air about him—motes of light that danced like fireflies in the grass. Whirling, circling, swooping, they drove round and round him, lighting the room with an eerie glow. Kor's eyes were open, his hands extended downward, his gaze fixed on the floor between and beneath them. It was toward this point that the milling motes of light were driven. Something was building there . . . something was taking shape from the blinking swarm that spiraled and swept downward and vanished into its growing, darksome bulk.

It took perhaps a minute. When he had concluded, a facsimile of the blistered corpse that had lain on Lord Roen Gol's terrace graced the plastic floor in front of him.


## 10.  UNDER ARREST


Safe again in his own quarters, Kor Danay carefully destroyed the Triszman garb he had worn, disassembling its structure, molecule by molecuel. That done, he bathed in a sparing amount of water and donned scarlet raiment once more. Then he rang for a tutor, and gave orders to fetch Brother Set.

"No doubt," he said abruptly as the Teacher entered his study, "you are surprised to see me still alive, Brother Set?"

The Blue Brother shook his round head. A faint smile twitched his lips. "I cannot say that I am, Sir Kor. Should I be?"

"If not surprised, then disappointed—or distressed . . . what is the word I am looking for?"

"Discomfited is probably the word you are groping for, Sir, but it is hardly appropriate. I am at a loss to supply a better."

The Sage glowered at the Teacher. "Brother Set, we may as well have it out now. Twice on my journey from the institute, you had me set upon with intent to kill . . ."

"Sir!" Brother Set's voice vibrated with shock.

"It will do no good to protest innocence. I scanned your image from the mind of the murderer you sent when your first pair of Thugs failed."

Brother Set chuckled. "I thought perhaps you had. You walked in here with a chip on your shoulder from the beginning. You must forgive me that slip, Sir. I had not much time after the Thugs returned with a tale of failure. I was obliged to act quickly, so I contacted the fellow in person."

"You don't deny it?"

"Did you expect a denial? Come, Sir Kor! So I have tried to have you killed! What is that between friends . . . *when we know that a Sage is practically unkillable by such methods?*"

Kor's eyes narrowed. "So you know that, do you? You are wrong; the Men *can* be killed. Tonight, for instance, I ran a very dangerous risk with my life. That I escaped is beside the point. You know that my Oath does not permit me to harm human life, unless my own is in danger. It seems to me that you are the biggest danger facing me at the moment, Brother Set."

"Kill me, then," the Blue Brother urged guilelessly, "if you believe it will free you of danger." He smiled his saintly smile. "After all, Sir, I merely carry out the orders of my civil superiors, who receive them directly from the Trisz. It is part of my duty to obey the Trisz and carry out the orders of the civil authorities. You have your oath and I have mine."

Kor scowled. "If you know your plots to kill me are bound to fail, why do you persist?"

Brother Set shrugged. "I am quite indifferent to that aspect of the situation, Sir. As I said, I merely act under orders. Those orders imply that you will be killed—and my duty is to assume that you will be."

"You have other plans, then?"

"Not I. You may as well know, Sir, that the situation

here is intolerable for you. It is not possible for you to remain alive. The Trisz have decreed death for you, and there is an end to the matter."

"How did the Trisz kill Sir Ten Roga?"

Again the Blue Brother shrugged. "I do not know."

"Where does Lord Roen Gol fit into this?"

"He was to have been charged with your murder and eliminated by public execution. His Lordship had begun to dabble in treason, and the Trisz have a predilection for their own kind of order."

"I was to be killed to afford an excuse for the legal murder of Lord Roen Gol? Then why the first two attempts, during my journey here?"

Brother Set yawned politely, covering his mouth with his hand. "I cannot answer all of your questions. After all, I am not a Sage. I am merely a Brother of the Order, attempting to carry out his duties."

Kor said, calculatingly, "You would have liked to be a Sage, wouldn't you?"

"Was I chosen? I serve well enough in my place."

"Indeed, you do. I can find no fault with your actions. I wonder only how much of what you seem to know about the Men has been communicated to the Trisz?"

Brother Set turned away. "Is that the reward for my discreetness? I have told them nothing. Suppose they suspected half as much as I, as you put it, seem to know?"

"Perhaps they do."

"Not likely. They would wipe you out to the last Man."

"Then why do they seek my life?"

"You have heard of the Extrapolator?"

The Sage remained silent, staring impassively.

"I assume you have," the Blue Brother went on, unperturbed. "The machine predicted your coming as a danger to the Trisz. You know that."

Kor did not deign an affirmative reply.

"The machine has made another utterance."

The Sage started. "It has?"

"Aha! I thought so!" Brother Set was again his genial, angelic self. "You would like to know what the machine says about you now, wouldn't you?"

Kor Danay drew himself up haughtily. "It makes no difference. I could pry the information out of you, if I chose."

"I believe you, Sir. Anybody who could sizzle and fry

one instant in the flames of six energy weapons, and the next be found running down the street with the murderers—"

"What do you know about that?"

"Not everything. I have heard that a fellow called Aln is missing. About your size, too. Some remembered that Aln joined them after the fracas, but he hasn't been seen since. I think it was you who joined the Thugs after the shooting."

"It was I." Kor paused, thinking. "Brother Set, I believe you when you say that the Trisz intend having me killed. There may be a way to defeat them. You can be with me or against me."

"As I suggested, Sir, you could kill me and obviate the question."

The Sage regarded Brother Set queerly. "I am sure you would not care if I did. But a Man cannot kill wantonly. If you attacked me, I could, and it would not violate my Oath. However, I should rather have you with me, Brother Set."

"I should prefer to be neither for you nor against you. Most of all, to remain alive!"

"What do you mean?"

"My own well-being requires that I serve my Masters, who are the Trisz. Can I serve you, too, and not be in danger from them?" He shuddered fastidiously. "I am sure you would have more compunction than they! Anyway, so far as I am concerned, you are as good as dead. I should gain nothing by serving you. But I may tell you one thing."

"And that is—?"

"The matter of the Extrapolator's prediction."

"I believe that it predicts my death."

"Indeed, yes. But some are worried by the terms in which the prognosis is couched."

"It is vaguely expressed?"

"Let me recite it for you." The Blue Brother closed his eyes, recollecting the pronouncement. "Here it is! *'The Sage will die undead; pots and pans depart, instead.'* Does it make sense to you, Sir?"

"It is a mess of contradictions! What is it to die 'undead'? Where do pots and pans fit into it?"

"That is just how the Trisz felt about it, Sir. Many times, however, the machine's pronouncements do not seem to bear the scrutiny of common sense—until after the event has come to pass."

"I should hope they made no sense of it," Kor interjected.

"Hope in vain, Sir. The Trisz have clearly realized the meaning of this bit of doggerel. They interpret it this way . . ." The Blue Brother paused, listened delicately, and smiled. "If I am not mistaken, Sir Kor—no, I am not—the Trisz soldiers are here now. It would be useless to tell you more!"

There was no opportunity to escape. The soldiers rushed into the room, weapons leveled. There was an uproar of stamping feet, barked commands. The soldiers surrounded Kor.

"You are under arrest, Sir Kor!" cried the officer.

Kor protested. "I claim the sanctuary of the Lodge! You cannot arrest me here."

The officer suddenly spied the weapon that Kor Danay had laid on a table. He picked it up, smiling grimly. "An energy weapon is contraband to any but the lawful guard of the Trisz. Your possession of it nullifies your resort to sanctuary. Will you come peaceably?"

Kor shrugged. "Very well. Put away your weapons."

Brother Set smiled with saintly pleasure as they led the Sage away.

The room in which they put Kor Danay was high up in the tower of the Administration Center. It measured hardly three paces one way by four the other, and there was not an item of furniture in it to relieve the monotony of smooth, colorless plastic. A dim light overhead cast the room into a fishbowl of pallid illumination.

As soon as the door was shut behind him, the Sage's submissive attitude vanished. He darted first to one wall and then to another, laying his palms against the cool, featureless plastic. He opened his mind, reached out just enough to penetrate the wall. Electrons swirled in his consciousness, flitting, flickering motes of seeming luminescence. Kor scanned the stream, poring over it, identifying, classifying, recording.

He found the energy weapon behind the rear wall without difficulty. It was rigged for remote control, and adjusted to spray the room with a broad cone of lethal radiation. He put his mind into the weapon, located the fuse that normally prevented overcharge of the circuit with consequent kickback on the operator. He carefully fused it to render the weapon useless.

With equal ease, Kor located the visor that watched him. It was hidden in the filament of the dimly burning lamp. It was complete with a microscopic pickup for sound. He closed his mind, dropped to his knees and began to chant aloud.

If ritual Remembrances could not bore the Trisz sufficiently, he thought, he could afford them other diversion later. Having finished his rites at last, Kor exercised briefly, wrapped himself in his scarlet cloak, lay down on the hard floor, and promptly fell asleep.

It must have been morning when the Sage awoke. In this windowless chamber, he could not tell whether the time was night or day, but he had mentally set himself for six hours of sleep, so it must be day by now. The dim lamp still burned overhead, and at the other end of the visio-audio hookup, doubtless, Triszmen still watched.

Kor performed the ceremonial Exercises of the Lodge, recited his morning Remembrances, then settled himself to await the Trisz' pleasure. When food was brought, he turned the bearer back at the door.

"A Man lives not by food alone," he pronounced. "Go— I have other matters to digest."

He carefully adjusted his metabolism to compensate for lack of sustenance, and continued to wait.

Shortly thereafter, the locking mechanism in the door whirred again. The guard ushered in a slovenly, middle-aged woman and clanged the door shut behind her.

"Are you the Man Kor?" she asked.

The Sage regarded her closely. Her lined cheeks sagged, and her eyes were puffed to mere slits. She wore a black kerchief over her hair. The saffron robe of a Triszman wrapped her.

She repeated, peering at him, "Are you the Man Kor?"

Kor Danay was wary, but he did not hesitate. He smiled and bowed politely. "I am the Man Kor," he replied.

"You aren't the Man I met at Roen Gol's!"

Kor's mind crept into the dimly glowing bulb overhead. He held the woman's gaze with his own, located the sight-and-sound pickup. Electrons swirled in his mind. He counted, selected two, turned a quadrant, and thrust. Overhead, one electron nudged another. A third dropped out of its orbit. The Trisz spy-device went dead.

Kor touched the woman's arm. He felt the instantaneous surge in every atom of his body as the time-stasis took hold. He freed the rigid air around them and stepped back, grinning. "You may come out of your disguise, Lady Soma!"

# 11.  CONDEMNATION

The Sage's pronouncement shocked his caller. She looked uncertainly at him and around the room.

Kor said, "We cannot be observed, so you can drop your disguise if you like. I have taken care of everything; just do not move from your position."

The dim ceiling light still glowed, its photo-vibrations altered to permit visibility within the zone of the time-stasis.

Suddenly she smiled and sighed. The puffed masses dropped from her eyes. Her cheeks grew firm and young. She straightened her shoulders. Her sea-green eyes sparkled at him. Kor looked and yearned for her.

"How did you know it was I?" Soma asked.

"I recognized the technique of your disguise," he said. "Sir Ten Roga must have taught you."

"He did. I know it's an elementary change, but it's the best I can do. Sir Ten said the Men can change their whole bodily structure at will, but he never demonstrated."

"True. A Man has full control over the individual molecules of his body-mass."

Soma became entirely practical. "Kor, I came here for one reason—to carry out the request you made last night, to convince the Trisz you are not the Man who attended my father's reception. I am supposed to identify you for the Triszmen. I asked to come."

"I guessed as much from your opening words. However, I am glad you are here. There are a few things I must know from you. Was your father arrested last night?"

"No. We planned in advance. Fast horses were ready. He escaped into the desert to join the Organization."

"What organization?"

"I cannot tell even you, Kor. Someday, you will find the Organization for yourself—if you live. I cannot entrust the knowledge to you . . . yet. If you can get out of this present situation . . ."

He shrugged the thought aside. "Tell me about yourself. You said you work on the staff of the Trisz Extrapolator. That can be very important."

She nodded vigorously. "I lead rather a double life. When I am not Lady Soma, I am Tasa Lanor, punch-card co-ordinator in the files section of the Extrapolator. It was as Tasa Lanor that I volunteered to meet you at the reception; you must have noticed that I kept my face hidden from the Thugs."

"I recall that you did. Very well. What about the Extrapolator? I hear it is a machine that predicts the future."

"Machine!" Lady Soma laughed shortly. "It is a monster! A brain, really. It occupies an entire building. Four hundred and eight floors are devoted to the mechanism alone, two hundred of them below ground level. Nearly a thousand floors are taken up with the technical staff, the clerical staff, the correlating division, the records division, the historical division, the traffic division, the scores of other divisions!"

"Rather a complex device for the mere purpose of holding the People subject, isn't it?"

"You mean— Oh, predicting riot, sedition, and plot isn't all the machine does! It's a mathematical computer of the highest order, and it thinks for itself. It really does. I couldn't name all the things it does, besides predicting the future. And of course, it isn't for Trisz use alone, either. It belongs to all the People. Anyone with a question about his future has the privilege of querying the Extrapolator. Many do. It's a part of the Trisz . . . benevolence."

"I suppose the machine disclosed your father's activities with the Lord of Set-loo?"

She nodded soberly. "Yes. When border fighting between my father's troops and the troops of Set-loo came to a halt, the information, with some other material, was fed to the machine. The civil authorities were excited by the machine's response and took it to the Trisz. The Trisz ordered my father's extermination along with yours."

"I am new to the ways of the world," Kor mused. "I cannot understand why the Trisz do not act as pleases them. Why they do not deal with their enemies on the spot, as it were."

"The Trisz like to maintain an appearance of benevolence. There is a semblance of self-rule among the People. The People are more easily kept in check if they do not realize too deeply that the Trisz are their masters. We still have law courts of our own that have not been tampered with, but these are only for dealing with common crimes among the People. When treason is the charge, the Trisz themselves are judge and jury, and the trials are conducted in secret. An excuse has to be found for the arrest—even if the Trisz have to manufacture an excuse. Like the energy weapon they claim to have found in your quarters."

"That was my own fault," Kor explained. "I was in possession of it. It is part of the story I have planned to tell at my trial."

Her shoulders sagged. "Do you know that they charge you with murder?"

"I rather expected they would. I have my defense ready."

"It will avail you nothing. Possessing the weapon sealed off your last excuse, if anything else were needed. It is death to possess one illegally."

"Then it would do me no good to plead innocent of murdering that fellow on your father's terrace?"

"Nor the other one whose body was discovered in a deserted house. Did you kill either of them? I—don't believe you did!"

She could not guess that the second body she referred to was only a duplicate of the first. As long as the Trisz did not suspect it, he was sanguine enough to believe he might win his freedom. Extrapolating the problem had done him no good. He could abstract nothing encouraging. He could only hope.

He said, "Soma, whatever you may hear in the future, I hope you will continue to believe my innocence, because such is the truth. On the other hand, I intend to confess to both murders!"

She did not change expression. "I do not question the wisdom of your actions, Sir Kor. Through Sir Ten and the Organization, I have learned to trust Men implicitly."

He tried to question her further about the Organization, but Soma shook her head, smiling tightly. "I have my Oath, too, Kor. Perhaps, if the Trisz . . ."

"Let me live?"

"I was about to say, have misinterpreted the machine's latest utterance concerning you."

The Sage quoted the jingle. "What does it mean 'die undead'? Can you tell me?"

"The Trisz think they know what it means. They take it both literally and metaphorically. The opinion is that you will quite literally die. They applied the word 'undead' to the machine for a semantic breakdown and got a complex variety of interpretations, from which they have made a tentative series of conclusions. Dead means no longer having life. Undead is not the opposite of dead, but is a condition of death. The result of a person suffering death is a dead body. A person suffering death and leaving no body is equally dead, but there is no 'dead' residue remaining. Do you see the implication?"

"They expected the concentrated blast of six energy weapons to reduce me to atoms," Kor put in. "No body would be left. But that did not happen—disregarding the identity of the body. The dead man fell behind the stone balustrade and was covered from the fire."

"Yes. So the Trisz knew immediately that you had escaped, if you were ever there. The fact did not coincide with the prediction, you see. They had their troops ready to close in on the Lodge to arrest you, knowing that if you did escape, you would go there immediately . . . as you did."

"I think I can guess my ultimate fate." He smiled grimly. "I am to be fed to the atomic converters in the power section of the city. That is a form of execution for condemned criminals, isn't it?"

She nodded, looking at him. He noticed how dark her eyes appeared. "Well, what about the pots and pans? Gibberish?"

She shook her head. "The machine never utters gibberish, but it frequently speaks metaphorically. 'Pots and pans' refers to the civil troubles the Trisz hope to prevent through their present action. The pots and pans departing idea is exemplified by my father's escape into the desert—a prediction, you see, that was not accurately interpreted at any time, until my father departed."

A stream of flashing electrons cut across the Sage's consciousness. The time-limit he had set was expiring.

He spoke almost cheerfully. "Time's up! Now remember. You came here to see if I am the Man who was at your father's reception."

"I am to report immediately after seeing you."

"You have already reported. There is a visio-audio spy device hidden in the filament of that lamp up there. It picked up the first words you uttered when you came in."

Soma's face paled. "You mean they have been listening?"

"They heard only your first words. How long do you think we have talked?"

"Five minutes—ten? Oh, no, it must be longer than that!"

"Considerably less than one-thousandth part of a second," he told Soma, with amusement. "In another thousandth of a second, the spy-device will become automatically reactivated, with none the wiser. Right now, we are outside of normal time. Before we go back, rearrange your disguise, and when I speak to you, continue as you started when you entered. We will again be under observation."

Electrons swirled in a mad dance of sparkling motes. Kor searched, located, identified, nudged electrons back into their places. "I am sure I never saw you before, Madame," he said respectfully.

The woman Tasa Lanor shrugged, looking him up and down. "Nor could I be mistaken about you, Sir."

She turned quickly to the door, banged on it with both fists.

Three days after his arrest, Kor Danay was notified of his trial. The Triszman officer who came to his cell was stern-visaged as he read the charges for the prisoner's benefit. The Sage listened in silence, and permitted himself to be led away to trial before the Trisz.

He faced his judge and accuser alone in a tiny chamber no larger than the one from which he had been taken, except that this room had a bay in one wall, in which the spindle-shaped Trisz vibrated a dull crimson, silent, inscrutable.

Television cameras had followed Kor to his reception, had focused on his back as he entered the Trisz chamber of justice. He knew that now an excited commentator was on the screen, recapitulating the Trisz version of the case for the benefit of watchers. None would see what went on within the chamber; none would know the story Kor Danay had to tell save the Trisz.

He braced himself against the hopelessness of the situation. The thin, reedy, mental "voice" of the Trisz cut across the Sage's consciousness.

"Man, you have heard the charges against you. Your own kind accuse you of dissidence, sedition, and treason against the Trisz. You are further accused of the murder of one Aln Darlon of the People, and of a Person unknown. You are charged as well with illegal possession of an energy weapon—a capital offense in itself. If you have anything to say before sentence is passed upon you, you may gesture for the recorders."

On one knee, Kor signed his reply. "I am innocent of these charges, O mighty Trisz—save that I did have in my possession the illegal weapon. Here is my defense:

"I received an invitation from the Lord Roen Gol, who will attest to the truth of this statement, to attend a reception in my honor. This is a function well established in custom, as the mighty Trisz know. Scorning transportation the short distance to his Lordship's residence, I decided to walk —"

Kor told his story straightforwardly, without a falter. He had, he said, about halfway to his goal, been set upon by two men, who overcame him and dragged him into a deserted house. There, he said, one of his captors stole his raiment, leaving his companion to guard him.

"From their talk," Kor explained, "I gathered that these two used this means to gain entrance to the estate in order to kidnap his Lordship's young daughter, to hold for ransom from her father."

Vigorously, then, the Sage gave an account of the fight he had had overpowering his guard. The weapon had been discharged in the struggle and his captor killed.

*So far, so good,* Kor thought. The Trisz had not wanted to admit their puzzlement over that second corpse. So now they had an explanation, which could only puzzle them the more.

He went on to relate that he had hastened to Lord Roen Gol's residence and had seen a woman on the terrace, struggling in the grip of one who was dressed in the scarlet garments of a Sage . . . undoubtedly his own. As he watched, the woman broke free and darted back inside.

"As I stood there, O mighty Trisz," Kor went on, "debating what to do, a sudden rain of energy whipped through the garden, engulfing the impostor in flames. My own captured weapon was also leveled. The noise of the other weapons startled me, so that unconsciously I depressed the firing stud, and the weapon fired.

"I therefore claim the benevolent protection of the mighty Trisz, and plead innocent to the charges of murder against me. The one man died by his own hand as I fought in self-defense, and the other was murdered by those who were obviously his accomplices in the kidnaping scheme, angered at seeing him allow Lord Roen's daughter to escape.

"As for the charges of dissidence, sedition, and treason, I can only plead innocent. And for possessing the weapon, I throw myself on the mercy of the Trisz, who can read from my mind the true occurrences as they happened."

"Man, there is evidence in your mind that what you say may be largely truth. You are a clever dissembler, however, and have learned how to mask your deepest thoughts. The Trisz are willing to dismiss the charges of murder, but your association with Lord Roen Gol, a known treasonist, and your possession of the weapon convict you of the remaining charges. These are crimes against the Trisz, whereas murder is a crime against the People. Crimes against the Trisz are punishable by death."

It was only what Kor had expected; he bowed his head.

"O benevolent Trisz," he gestured, "I have but one further request to make."

"Speak, Man."

"I ask that my body be returned to the Institute for burial in that sacred ground."

The Trisz hummed thoughtfully. "That is impossible, Man. The course of execution is set by expedience and custom. You will die instantly and painlessly, in complete dissolution of your physical body. There will be nothing left to bury."

Kor paced his cell, his mind busy with his problem. In spite of the Trisz verdict, he had no feeling of the imminence of dissolution. He was in peril, certainly. But the future did not appear to hold death. If this were so, then deliverance was still to come. He seized upon this thought and submitted it to the third-order processes of his mind. He heaved a sigh and relaxed. Of course. The time had not yet come for his need to assert itself. At present, he was safer here than he could be anywhere else. He had only to wait —wait for the eleventh hour.

Scarcely an hour passed before the Sage was removed from his cell, prodded into an elevator, and dropped swiftly he knew not how many levels below the surface. Two officers accompanied him. They were met at the bottom level by three guards with drawn weapons. The five surrounded Kor Danay and conducted him down a long corridor to a pneumatic tube-car station. They got into the waiting tube car, which shot away, then slowed to a stop in a matter of seconds.

He disembarked in the eye-searing blaze of illumination that encompassed the city's heart. Great machines arrayed themselves as far as he could see in every direction. A forest of pillars, girdered and trussed, supported the roof of this artificial cavern. Everywhere, the machines that fed life to the city hummed, shot sparks, emitted a strong odor of ozone.

A score of uniformed, armed guards were waiting. The officers and guards who had accompanied him returned to their tube car. Kor was marched through the maze of machinery until he stood before a leaden wall, studded with meters, dials, and great doors that looked like the breech-blocks of monster cannon. All along the wall, chain conveyors, one to each door, rattled in starts and jerks. As the nearest conveyor jerked forward, a thick lead door swung open . . . the chains rattled in with a load of trivia . . . the door swung shut. Farther away, another door opened, the conveyor jerked and rattled. Up and down the length of this endless wall, the process repeated itself intermittently, the conveyors feeding the ravening atomic converters that filled the veins, arteries, and nervous system of this great city with the vibrant power of its artificial life.

Each time a door opened, the Sage noticed, the dial above it dropped to zero. As the door closed on a load of waste, the needle jumped upward, registering the last quantum of energy released from its dissolution. He knew that when his own body was fed to this vast, unfriendly machine, that needle would leap again, registering the amount of energy released from the atoms of his body. Somewhere, a recording machine would take note of the amount with an arrangement of perforations on a tape. That was all that would remain of the Man Kor: an arrangement of holes on a very brief length of tape.

He was not insensible, either, to the occasion that was being made of his execution. Already the news of his condemnation had been broadcast, and every eye in the city was turned to the televisor screens. Television cameras peered at the Sage silently from a dozen angles.

Kor held himself rigidly erect. He was a Man. He had no plan, except to submit to whatever lay in store for him. He would die like a Man, if need be. *Need.* Again he heard the voice of Val Shan monotonously intoning the Oath held precious by the Scarlet Sages . . . *"I solemnly vow never to use my powers against any of the Trisz . . . though I lose my life . . ."*

Men had died before at the behest of the Trisz. To dart away now, as Kor Danay longed to do, would betray the Brotherhood; worse, betray the very People to whom the Brotherhood of Men was dedicated, and Earth too.

A conveyor had been switched from automatic to manual. It stood moveless and ready. Naked to the waist, the Sage was led to it, stretched out on the cold chains and lashed fast. Kor looked up into a blaze of light and the snout of an unblinking, emotionless, television camera. On the other side of that lens, a million People watched. He imagined their stir of feelings, and he smiled.

A smartly uniformed officer paced to the Sage's side. He read sententiously from a sealed and beribboned document.

"Kor Danay, of the Brotherhood of Men, formerly Man of the Chapter of No-ka-si, you have been examined and found guilty of crimes against the Trisz; to wit, dissidence, sedition, treason, and illegal possession. For these offenses, Trisz justice requests the death penalty, to be administered humanely, without pain or physical suffering, by dissolution in the atomic converter. You are permitted to beg forgiveness of your God for your crimes before the sentence is carried into execution."

Kor lifted his head. "I have made my peace with my God," he said quietly.

The officer folded the paper smartly and stepped back a pace. "May your God have mercy on your soul, Sir Kor!"

## 12.  ". . . POTS AND PANS DEPART . . ."

The officer lifted his hand. Kor Danay turned his glance toward the great leaden door. Slowly, it began to swing open, exposing the shining interior. The officer brought his hand down.

The conveyor jerked, ground forward. The Sage's naked back slid along the smooth metal runway. His mind raced. Another instant, and he would be inside. Too late then . . . He *was* inside. The door would swing shut. Far too late . . . It *swung* shut. He was enclosed in coffin-like darkness, bound to the silent chains. In another instant, dissolution—to be followed by the leap and fall of the needled dial above the door. The door would open again upon an empty chamber, readied for another load of garbage . . .

In his mind's eye, the Sage could see the dramatic focusing of the television screens on that meter. He would need

. . . *Need!* Kor snapped himself into the time-stasis—reached out exploringly with his mind. Already, the current had begun to flow in the arm-thick leads that fed the giant bus bars of the converter. He could sense the sluggish flow of it from atom to atom, from molecule to molecule . . .

Even in time-stasis, he had precious little time. The flow of current into the converter was practically instantaneous in normal time. Again the Extrapolator's jingle went through his mind: *"The Scarlet Sage will die undead, pots and pans depart, instead."* A silly, dancing refrain. *Desire. Need. Resolve. Will. Now* was the need—*now* was the time! It became clear in a flash. Here was his destiny, to be accomplished in the split fraction of a second required for the surging current to activate the converter. No eye could see him, the energy field of the converter would mask his own field as he hurled himself to the ends of the Universe. None would be the wiser!

None the wiser? How about that telltale dial with the television cameras focused upon it? How about the quanta of released energy to be recorded?

*Pots and pans!*

The Sage focused his mind upon his own body. Electrons streamed thick and fast through his consciousness. He weighed, counted, evaluated every physical element of which his body was composed. He would have to replace every molecule with an equivalent molecule of other matter. He cast his mind out, out of that deathtrap, instantaneously, into homes and public eating places. The stress he made in the sub-ether, which the Trisz might have detected, was completely masked by the energy field set up in the converter.

Pots and pans! There were scores of them, thousands of them to be had! Mysteriously, from a kitchen here, from a kitchen there throughout the city, pots and pans vanished. Other items, too—water, sand from the desert—a perfect assortment of heterogeneous matter, equivalent in its sum to the energy-mass of Kor Danay's physical body.

He remembered a place, a small, quadrangular area before the dais of the Lodge, where he had remained one day to meditate. He had practiced molecular dissection of it then, and now that dissection remained with him. He had no time to select a place more suitable or less dangerous; he must go there at once. The sluggishly flowing current already caressed the discharge cathodes. His mind grasped the functions of dissimilarity.

All over the city, the People stood or sat transfixed before televisor screens, eyes glued to the image of a moveless needle. The needle jerked over suddenly, and a great sigh went up—as assorted pots, pans, and other junk materialized in the converter and took the dissolution intended for the Sage.

Kor Danay stood with head bowed before the dais of the Lodge, a half-naked Man who had met—and mastered—the Trisz.

He dared hesitate only a second. The Lodge seemed deserted, but he could not risk having a tutor blunder in and discover him. He hurried to his own quarters, let himself into his study.

"I thought perhaps you would return here first."

Kor jerked around. Brother Set sat cross-legged on the floor, smiling his saintly smile. "I must say, though," he went on, "that it has been a tiring vigil. I could not know precisely when you would get here."

The Sage stood poised, speechless. He eyed the Blue Brother with a calculating intensity. "You expected this?" he said at last. "Is this another prelude to an invasion by Trisz soldiers? You know they cannot take me now!"

"Perish the thought!" Brother Set wagged his head. "How may I convince you, Sir Kor, of my delight at witnessing your evasion of Trisz justice? I have been for you all along, if only you knew it."

The Sage cast his mind in a cautious circle, exploring the surroundings. Brother Set spoke the truth. There were no soldiers within a mile, and even the Lodge itself was deserted, save for them. Normal conditions of life prevailed in the town, as far as Kor dared reach out.

"What is loyalty?" The Blue Brother queried sagely. "Is it not love for one's own skin? Such has been my loyalty to the Trisz."

"You did not offer to help me," Kor pointed out.

"Can the buried help the living? A Man is necessarily his own help, Sir Kor. What could I have done that you could not—save to further those plans destined to give you your freedom? And now that you are both dead and undead, Sir, what is your next move? Well, never mind answering. You do not fully trust me."

Brother Set looked unhappy. The Sage laughed sharply. "You have been a strange sort of friend, if not an audacious enemy, Brother Set. How can one who has proved himself a villain become worthy of trust? But perhaps I can trust

73

you this far . . . to get me clothing such as is worn by the People. I dare not appear again in public dressed as a Man."

Brother Set got painfully to his feet, shook the cramps out of his legs. "Under the circumstances, a public appearance would be rather dangerous for you. I suggest flight, myself. As for clothing, you will find what you need in there." He nodded toward a massive chest against the wall.

Kor gave him a piercing look. The chest had contained his own wardrobe of Brotherhood garments, he well knew. He stepped quickly to the chest, lifted the lid.

A complete outfit of common clothing lay neatly folded on the very top. Kor lifted the topmost piece, a coarse brown material of fluffy texture that would insulate from the sun as well as keep out the cold. He turned to the Blue Brother. "You *did* expect me to return!"

"I hoped for the best, let us say. You will note that the color of the garments will pass wherever you may go. You could be a farmer from the Mis-pi with those clothes, or a desert wolf in for a holiday. You will find identification papers in the pocket . . . a clever forgery, if I do say so myself, who committed the crime."

The Sage relaxed and grinned, then sobered quickly. "I do not trust you that far, Brother Set. Forgive my seeming suspicion if I change the identification you have so thoughtfully provided. The Sages are rather clever at forgery themselves. I will take care of the matter before leaving. My thanks now, Brother; you may leave me alone."

The Blue Brother turned to go.

"Brother Set!"

"Yes, Sir Kor?"

"Tranquillity, Brother."

"Tranquillity, Sir!"

Alone, Kor Danay studied the document. Brother Set may have been in earnest, but the Sage could afford to take no chances. The paper was printed, with appropriate blanks for filling in desired information with a pen. He put his mind into the paper, deftly erased the hand-written parts by freeing the molecules of ink from the paper. With equal care, he replaced the molecules in a pattern of his own, giving himself a different name, place of origin and age. The age he chose was sixty-five.

A half-hour later, a burly, gray-bearded fellow dressed in the coarse, brown habiliments of an Outlander, passed down the steps of the Lodge and disappeared into the night that lay heavily over No-ka-si. None but another Man would have recognized that figure.

The inn was crowded and noisy. A stuffy pall of rancid cigar smoke and the reek of synthetics hung heavily on the air. Kor made his way among the tables, listening sharply as he went. He paused by a table seating four young Triszmen.

Kor sat down nearby and ordered a mug of synthetic.

"These Lodge Men aren't so upright," one sounded off. "I tell you they aren't for the People at all. That goes for the Reds and the Blues both. I think they're constantly working against the Trisz, and we're the ones who'll suffer."

The Sage let his mind steal out. He located the spy devices hidden in the walls. He wanted that young man, but here was no place to interfere with him. Kor lifted his mug from time to time as if to drink from it. The level of the liquid went down, but none of it passed Kor's lips.

Meanwhile, the Sage's mind was subtly busy. One by one, the talker's companions found an urgent need to be elsewhere. When the last one had departed, Kor planted a compulsion in the remaining Triszman's mind to go home; the fellow got to his feet and weaved out of the inn. After a minute, Kor followed him out.

Kor had left the Lodge with a decision to find the "organization" Soma Gol had mentioned. To do that, he felt, he must locate the girl, and the only way to find her was to seek her in the vicinity of the Extrapolator. Instinctively, he had been led to the inn where his path would cross that of this employee of the Operating Section.

How simple if he could have found Soma by this same method. But the situation was not the same.

Trailing a burst of ribald song, the technician turned a corner and staggered down a repulsively dark side street. Kor overtook him rapidly. He seized the Triszman by his saffron cloak, forced him back against the wall of a dark building. There was no struggle. The technician collapsed under the sudden fierce probe of the Sage's mind into his conscious faculties. Quickly, the Sage drained his quarry's mind of the information he needed. Satisfied, Kor turned back, found the main thoroughfare leading to Ka-si, and walked along it.

Lights sped up from the rear and passed him, crossing beams with those that came townward from the city. An empty surface car passed, rolled to a halt at Kor's hail.

"Yes, sir! Just got in tonight," Kor gaffed pleasantly with the driver. "I've made my pile, young feller, and now I'm looking for a place to have fun. Know any?"

The driver was a mine of information. He expected a generous tip from this garrulous old Outlander with gray beard and obviously new clothing. The fellow was quick to offer suggestions, comparisons, and recommendations with a hearty gusto.

"Well," Kor wheezed in his old man's voice, "drop me somewhere convenient to all of 'em, youngster!" He cackled at his own low joke. "No sense in playin' favorites!"

Kor knew what was expected of him. Upon leaving the car, he tipped generously from the fund of money Brother Set had thoughtfully left in a pocket of his suit. The driver had been a help in establishing his fictitious identity. The watchers on the other end of the car's spy devices had a record of him now, sufficiently banal to put them at ease.

The crowd was thick on the avenue. Music blared from the television screens, which depicted writhing dancers posturing and flinging themselves in time with a rapid, insensate rhythm. The Sage paused, pretending interest. He was a "rube," and everything the city had to offer must seem an amazement and a delight to him. He lost himself quickly in a swirl of colorful garments that flowed around him.

Kor let himself be carried casually in the direction he wanted to go. It was not far. The Extrapolator was centrally located, housed in a tall spire of rainbow-hued plastic. Its base-area was tremendous, surrounded by a quarter-mile extent on every side by gardens. Kor hurried along a deserted path under the trees. He had been "executed" at sunset; the hour was still early evening. The Extrapolator would be available to the public for several hours yet.

Mile-broad steps led up to an equally long row of open doors. People were going in and out, singly and in groups; bright garments flashed in the artificial light.

Colorful, lighted posters and placards caught the Sage's attention.

*What's Tomorrow?* said one. Another read, *Happiness Is His Who Knows. See What Tomorrow Holds Before Acting Today!*

Kor went in, asked directions of a uniformed attendant, and proceeded to the Prediction Center. He walked heavily, as an old man should.

A badly made-up young woman with a nasal whine to

her voice halted him at the reception desk. "Your name, please?"

He gave her the fictitious identity he had assumed. "Sam Nodel."

"Your papers, please."

Kor brought out his identification. It was plain that the Prediction Center, available to and used by all the People as it was, was a first-class Trisz checking station on the activities, desires, and aspirations of the citizens.

"How old are you?"

Kor thrust a gnarled finger at the paper. "It tells . . . right there."

She looked into his face with a vacuous stare. "How old are you, please?"

"Sixty-five."

She checked the statement against the paper. "Your birth date?"

Kor told her.

She went over every scrap of information on the paper, requiring him to give the information orally. The Sage knew that out of sight, a silent recording machine was taking down his replies, timing his reaction. He gave everything smoothly, just right.

"What is your question, please?"

Kor attempted to evade. "I—I am looking for someone."

"The Extrapolator does not locate missing persons."

"Uh . . . no. I want to know if I will meet this person again."

"That is better. Enter cubicle 3-C as soon as the present occupant leaves. State your question clearly and completely. All questions are recorded. The machine will give you an answer immediately."

She thrust his papers at him and he moved away. The door of cubicle 3-C opened and a Triszman came out. Kor entered quickly. There was a low bench in the cubicle, fronted by a table. He sat down, folded his arms on the table top.

A voice rasped at him, "Ten seconds! Formulate your questions in ten seconds, please!"

Ten seconds passed slowly. The Sage stared impassively at the wall. There was no equipment in the cubicle. The voice said, "State your question, please."

"Under what circumstances will I meet Tasa Lanor again?" Kor voiced the question slowly, distinctly.

The machine was quiet a moment. Then the voice spoke again. "Question rejected on the basis of insufficient directives. You have ten seconds in which to reformulate the question."

He wrestled for a half-hour with the machine's obtuse noncomprehension of his affair. The Lady Soma had told him that all local information was fed to this machine. Therefore, the name of Tasa Lanor was a part of the machine's knowledge. It could not tell him what it knew, only what it might predict from the basis of its knowledge. Sufficient directives had to be supplied to route the machine correctly toward making a proper prediction.

Finally, the voice from the machine spoke again: "Your prediction is ready. There is paper and pencil on the table. You may write it down."

The machine uttered its singular pronouncement. Kor stared at what he had written. *At the first hour of morn, when the Sun is born, an old man stumbles, 'twixt love and duty torn.*

He wondered if it were possible for a machine to be insane, then shrugged, tucked the slip of paper in his pocket and left the Prediction Center. The meaning depended upon whether the verse were uttered factually or metaphorically. He made a rational third-order analysis of the situation, and decided to accept the factual interpretation.

He would await Tasa Lanor in the park outside this building at the first hour of morn.

The sun lifted a swollen, bloody face over the sleeping city. Kor Danay had held his post since the first break of dawn, watching the crowds of People as the working shift changed. Obviously, crews were on duty around the clock, and Soma's shift began at sunrise.

Just as the Sun came up, he saw her walking swiftly through the park, in the guise of Tasa Lanor. She was alone. Kor moved quickly, made sure with special senses that it was she. "Tasa Lanor," he said, touching her arm.

The touch informed her. She looked at him with wide, startled eyes. "Kor!"

Gladness touched her face, curved her lips. Her disguise began to drop away. "Watch it!" he cautioned. "Take hold of yourself. It is I, Kor."

She brought her hands to her face, stood shuddering and sobbing. At last she looked up at him; she had recovered

78

her composure. "It is truly you! I—I thought . . . I saw . . ."

"I know. You saw the broadcast of my execution. It is enough to say that I escaped. I had to see you."

Her grip was firm on his arm, but her voice trembled. "Kor—Kor, I'm so glad!"

He said, "We mustn't talk too long. Quickly: How can I get to the Organization?"

She drew in her breath. "I—I can't tell you—now. I have to check first."

Exasperation seized him. He could not forget the prediction, *"an old man stumbles."* He got a grip on himself.

"Look, Soma! I dare not return to the Institute except that they are prepared for my coming. And I have to leave here on foot. It is dangerous to use my powers even a little here in the city. You must get me to the Organization. . ."

"I know—and I will. Tomorrow. Meet me here."

Heavy boots thudded on the pavement. Kor turned casually away.

A sharp voice cried, "Halt!"

Kor looked into the unsmiling face of an officer of the Trisz guard. He was blocked by a squad of armed, uniformed guardsmen.

"What is your name, please?"

Kor's gray beard trembled with just the proper amount of agitation. "Sam Nodel. I—I'm a stranger here. What is the meaning of this?"

The officer turned his cold attention to Soma. "You are Tasa Lanor?"

She nodded.

"You are both under arrest, in the name of the Trisz. Please come with me.

*So this was the outcome,* Kor thought. Of course, his questions last night had been scanned by the suspicious enemy. It is the virtue of a conqueror to be suspicious.

## 13. THE ORGANIZATION

The Commander of the Guard at the precinct station was cool and pleasantly polite.

"You understand, of course," he smiled, "that this is

merely a security check. It is required for the records that a complete dossier be made of the relationship between you two. Miss Lanor is a government employee, and you, sir, are from the Outlands. If you will just answer a few questions . . ."

It was ridiculously easy—a simple exercise in advanced hypnosis. Kor took over the mind of the Triszman officer, impressed upon it a complete array of false information. He topped it off with a legitimate desire to permit this harmless couple to go their way. The two were released with the same smiling courtesy with which they had been received.

"I cannot now return to my job," Soma told Kor afterward. "Whatever use I may have been to the Organization is ended. The Trisz have an intricate system of records, and you can be sure they are being scanned from every angle. Your own identity is being traced. We have perhaps half an hour before the entire Trisz guard will be ordered out to search for us."

"Then let us go to the Organization at once."

"Are you mad? We could not even leave the city!"

"I can manage that," Kor said quietly.

She looked at him with sudden hope. Kor smiled wryly. "I stumbled all right, when I made a public show of myself meeting you. But it is you who are *'twixt love and duty torn.'* "

"What are you talking about?"

He gave her the penciled prediction. She looked up at him again, eyes darkly brooding. "I cannot take you directly to the Organization without authorization and directions. I may as well tell you, the Organization expected to receive you if you successfully avoided the Trisz kind of justice. But I have taken an Oath to suffer death before revealing the location of the Organization to anyone. And that includes unauthorized Sages, Sir Kor."

"The Scarlet Sage is dead," he assured her. "I am Kor—none other. The Scarlet Sage was executed yesterday at sunset by order of the Trisz. Have you forgotten? If the Organization expects to receive me, we had better hurry."

"You are dead—and yet you live? How can I be sure that you are the Man Kor? I feel that you are, it is true. But what proof have I? If you are actually a Triszman, you would come armed with any knowledge Sir Kor may have had. If you live, you must have broken your Oath—and that I cannot believe of a Sage!"

"You misunderstand." Kor tried to be patient. "I did not use my powers against the Trisz, nor could the field I set up be detected by them. Under cover of the static generated by the converter, I escaped through subspace, to the Lodge in Ka-si. From there, I made my way here in search of you."

Her glance darted at him.

"Did you see anyone at the Scarlet Lodge?"

"I saw Brother Set."

"What did he say?" The question was abrupt, eager.

"He said," Kor laughed, " *'I thought you would return here first.'* "

She fell into his arms, hugged him, squeezing his arms with her fingers, laughing and crying, "Kor—Kor! It truly is you!"

"Of course it is I. But what—?"

She looked up at him. There were tears in her eyes. "Don't you see yet? Brother Set is one of us! He would have said what he did only to the real Kor; he *was* expecting you! . . . Now, if you can get us out of the city, I will take you to the Organization!"

The Sage performed in a deserted section of the park fronting the Extrapolator. They sat side by side on a stone bench, in the shelter of some sparse shrubbery, and Kor put his mind to work. A few minutes later, two wholly different identities strolled casually out of the garden—an affectionate young couple, arm in arm, with eyes and thoughts for nothing in the world save each other. Only a Sage who knew both would have recognized Kor Danay and the Lady Soma in their transmutational disguises.

Deep in the rocky core of the mountains near Den-ver, a great cavern blazed with light and hummed with activity. This was a secret lair of the Organization—one of its lairs. There were others around the world, in isolated territories, each deeply buried in the earth and thoroughly shielded from the remotest chance of discovery.

There was no way into such a retreat as this, and no way out. No tunnels led to the surface, to betray its location with their open mouths. Only the Scarlet Sages attached to the Organization knew about the buried cities and knew how to operate the matter transporters that brought people and materials in, and rarely let them out.

The Organization, Kor learned from Soma, represented the "underground" activity of the Men. Those graduates who distinguished themselves in worldly service were transferred here after a pretense of dying and being buried. Men and women of the People were also spirited into the underground cities to work with the Men. In this manner, over the centuries, the populations of the buried cities had grown, until some, like Sub-den, to which Soma led Kor, were enormous in extent.

The buried cities were each an individual world of its own, having no connection with the surface. The only ones who might leave, once they had entered, were those Sages dispatched to secret duty outside, or in the farthest depths of space.

He had hardly been aware of entering the cavern. He had stood with Soma in a dry gulch an hour's ride into the desert from Ka-si. She had motioned with her hands a secret signal, and suddenly they stood in a rock-walled chamber miles away and under ground.

"Where I took you," Soma told him, "is one of the 'lifting places' on which the matter transporters are constantly trained. I have been here many times, but never farther into the city than this reception room. Here I talked with the Commander of the Organization, and then I was sent back to the lifting place. That is all I can tell you. I learned of the Organization through Sir Ten Roga, who was a trusted and valuable member. He brought me here and I was initiated into the role of spy for the Men." She shrugged. "There will be no more of that for me now. I cannot again appear as Tasa Lanor, and my father's authority no longer exists. I am hoping that the Men will find a place for me here."

A door opened in the rocky wall and a sleek-looking young woman came out. She was obviously a woman of the People, slim and lithe, her skin a deep bronze. Her eyes were dark brown, and sparkled in keeping with her smile. "Come in, please. The Commander is waiting for you."

Kor ushered Soma ahead of him. Both had re-established their own physical identities.

The erect, Olympian figure behind the desk held out both hands. "Welcome, Sir Kor. And Lady Soma!"

"Val Shan!"

Kor strode happily forward, seized the Master's hand.

Val Shan smiled. "You gave us rather a difficult time, Kor," he reproved. "You moved too fast for us to keep pace with you!"

Kor grinned wryly. "I was living fast, Sir!"

"Sit down, both of you," Val Shan invited cordially. "Kor, tell me about it. Speak with perfect frankness before

Soma. She may as well start her indoctrination as a future citizen of Sub-den."

Kor launched into his story, sparing no details, but it was obvious that many of the explanatory terms, commonplace to himself and Val Shan, were utterly foreign words to Soma's ears. He concluded with the account of their arrest and escape.

Val Shan's thoughts seemed to be fixed a great distance away. "Conduct befitting a Man, Kor," he murmured at last.

Kor swelled with pride. "Thank you, Sir!"

"However," Val Shan frowned, "I had hoped that affairs would take a slower pace. Your return has been a little too soon."

"Too soon, Sir?"

Val Shan waved his hand. "Never mind." He peered at his interlaced fingers on the gleaming desk top. "Kor, I have a great deal to tell you, now that you are 'dead.' Does it bother you that I use that term? . . . No? Well, I had hopes you might have gotten a little closer to the Trisz than you did. You might have cleared up, perhaps, a few points that are still beyond our present knowledge. But that is beside the point. We had extrapolated your adventure, of course, but something was awry with our equations. We obviously did not have enough directives. At any rate, our extrapolation didn't come close to the actual events."

He leaned back in his chair and faced them both squarely.

"From now on," said he, "both of you must remain residents of Sub-den. Therefore, I am going to tell you what we are doing here, and why we are doing it. Obviously, Kor, we could not teach you at the Institute about the underground activities of the Men. Not all of the Men know about our Organization. Only those deemed most worthy and useful are finally let in on the secret and brought here to further the work. Your own case was decided before you left the Institute. There is a place here for your divisible mind. We want a chance to study it—and to let you use it."

He paused, opened a drawer in the desk, drew out a gilded humidor of scented cigars. Kor refused. Val Shan selected a cigar and momentarily focused his attention on its tip; it issued a tiny flame. He drew in a lungful of smoke.

"There is more to the work of the Men, of course, than merely following an idealistic principle of someday freeing Mankind from the yoke of the Trisz." He paused, frowned into the wreathing whorls of cigar smoke, and continued. "If it were not for the Trisz, we would be masters of the Universe. I mean that quite literally. And the rest of mankind, and the other intelligent species throughout the Universe, would be a hundred thousand years advanced beyond their present state of civilization.

"Let us take a look at this Universe. What is its fundamental nature? In rough analogy, it is like scales in a state of balance. Its equilibrium is determined as much by those forces which seek, to use a metaphorical expression, to lift it up as to those which desire to tear it down. That which is in the Universe balances itself against that which is not. The positive arrays itself against the negative. Tomorrow asserts itself against today. In very ancient times, this continual, two-way struggle of the Universe was dimly recognized. Our ancestors saw in this constant effort toward balance a struggle between what they called Good and Evil.

"To couch our present situation in these ancient terms, we would say that the forces of Good—the Men—are confronted by the forces of Evil—the Trisz. Statements such as this once passed among men as rational, but we now recognize that such a statement is not even good semantics.

"The Men are not good, in any sense that the term might imply. Neither are the Trisz evil. In fact, from the viewpoint of the Trisz, the entire set of values would be reversed. Do you understand what I am getting at?"

His two listeners nodded, but Kor was puzzled.

Val Shan continued, sketching a broad picture of the Universe as not a place or an expanse, but an ideation only.

"The idea which is our Universe," Val Shan told them, "is one that is apprehended by mind. It is an intellectual concept, if you like the term better. Our own awareness apprehends that the Universe exists. If it requires awareness to apprehend this existence, then awareness was required to establish it. That is as far as human reasoning will go. Beyond this point, our method of third-order rationalization takes us to the ultimate answer to the question of the constitution of the Universe. This answer is not on the verbal level. It is apprehended only in the mind, and fully, only in the minds of the Men.

"Even in very ancient times, the mind of man apprehended this ultimate answer. Once, uncounted millennia ago, before the Brotherhood of Men ever rose out of the pit of darkness into which the pre-Men plunged the world, there lived One who said, *The world shall pass away, but my words shall not pass away.'* We have His words today. And He once said to a questioner, *'Why callest thou me good? None is good, save one, and that is God.'* "

In those times, Val Shan went on to explain, the concept of Good consisted of that which was in the People's favor; and what was Evil was that which worked to their detriment.

"What was God to those ancient men? God was the epitome of Good. Everything which was right and proper for men came from God. There is only one Good, and that is for both men and the Trisz to recognize. We, the Men, know that the Trisz do not comprehend this principle; it is completely alien to their understanding. Because of the alien aspect of the principle to Trisz understanding, we can have hope that ultimately we shall destroy him, because we understand the principle and know how to use it—as the People of the Universe could have used it thousands of years ago with the first coming of the enemy—if they had known about it."

Val Shan's listeners hung on his words. "Good is for him who avails himself of it. It is an enormous power that is available to all. I have loosely called it 'Good,' a third-order rationalization, which cannot be abstracted to the verbal level.

"The effect of the principle, however, is this, that the balance must maintain itself in the Universe. No force can gain headway in a given direction without an opposing force falling back. When the opposing force returns, then the other must give way. That is the law. There is no such thing as an irresistible force or an immovable object.

"What has this to do with our present state of affairs in the Universe? The People of the Universe are all of a kind, spiritually speaking.

"On worlds everywhere, civilization rose, attained a high state of technological advancement, then fell in ruins. The spiritual force which was man, in the idea of inhabitants of the Universe, if it could not advance, neither could it remain in one place. It had to fall back before an opposing force. The Trisz, wherever they came from, supplied that force. In so short a time that it was almost instantaneous, man was pushed back on all fronts. The Trisz had the ascendancy . . . and they have maintained it to this day. The Trisz, in complete command of the Universe, are slowly destroying it by a subtle process of squeezing out all other forms of life.

"It is doubtful," the Master pointed out, "if the Trisz themselves realize this fact, though they may understand it without realizing its conclusion. If the balance of the Universe is not restored by a return movement of Mankind, the People will finally disappear. There will be only one force left—the Trisz—and they and the Universe will perish!"

"I do not understand," Soma put in. "The Universe is a matter of atoms, molecules, planets, suns, galaxies! What has the spiritual struggle between the Trisz and the Men to do with all this? The Universe cannot be changed!"

Val Shan smiled. "The Universe changes every second, my dear. Every passing moment charts its future more completely, more surely. It is doctrine with the Men that the future is established, but it is also doctrine that the future can be changed. What is the future, after all? Is it not the sum of past events, manifested in the transpiration of phenomena, each having its roots in the phenomena of the past? What you will do tomorrow depends upon what you do today . . . as today's deed depends upon yesterday's action . . . and so on back to the beginning of time."

"If this is so," she put in, "the future is set by the actions of the past. How can it be changed without changing the past?"

"You speak of actions and of the past as if they were concrete objects, fixed forevermore," Val Shan chided her gently. "This is not true. Remember what I said about the Universe and all it contains being not an expanse, not a space, not material, even, but an ideation? The Universe is the creation of a Mind vaster than anything you may conceive.

"Today's events pass quickly into the past and become a part of it, subtly altering the future probability from the shape it obtained yesterday. Each day that passes alters the future more and more. It is conscious, intelligent effort directing today's events that produces the change desired in tomorrow's happenings.

"Let us consider that potent tool possessed by the Trisz: technology. See what they have done with it. Lacking hands to control the implements of their science, they have obtained hands to work for them. Their technology—and behind it, their mental acumen or ability for technology—provided them with the tools and expedients of conquest and victory.

"On the other hand, the Men now have a technology as far-reaching as that of the Trisz, even diverging from theirs in some aspects. It is being used in this and similar caverns all over the livable Universe . . . wherever the problem of destroying the Trisz confronts the race of Men. But beyond their technology, the Men have something else which the Trisz have not and can never hope to have. They have faith, hope, and aspiration—and the ultimate knowledge that there is only one Good, and that is God!"

Val Shan settled back with a deep sigh. "Well, that is the general picture. You will both receive further indoctrination and training in specialized lines of conduct." He turned to Soma. "For you, my dear, a place has been made in the integrating section of our Search Division. That is the home-office force, so to speak, of the Searchers who are continuously combing space for habitable worlds, and the ultimate home of the Trisz, wherever it may be."

He directed his attention to Kor. "We have no place into which you will easily fit, Kor. But I have a word for you alone." He nodded to Soma. "You may go now. The young woman in the outer office will take care of you."

When Soma had gone, Val Shan turned again to Kor.

"You may have wondered why we offered you no help once you had left the Institute. It would have been a case of the blind leading the blind. You had to be left to your own resources in order to further those developments we were seeking. It is of greater advantage to one to learn to explore a region as he perceives it through his own apprehension. You see what I mean: your whole training as a Man was founded on the principle of self-learning with guided direction. At a given point, the direction had to be removed in order for you to supply your own."

"Yes, sir," Kor agreed. "You mean I had to develop faith in myself."

"And several other qualities," Val Shan returned ambiguously. "You know that the impingement of the element of self upon scientific investigation has not been decreased more than a trifle by the training and regimen of the Men. Keep that thought in mind. What we want and what is are two totally different objectives. The subjective mixing of them has always caused difficulty through crippling the scientist's ability to observe and react properly to his observations.

"Beware the philosopher who tells you, *'Think!'* and invariably adds, parenthetically and under his breath, *'Like me!'* It is from this fundamental error of procedure that the Men have tried to free their reason. I think like Val Shan; you think like Kor Danay. We do not have to think alike in order to arrive at the same objective conclusion. In mathematics, it is the method that counts. As Men, we are concerned with conclusions, and the method can go hang! You cannot think as I do, any more than you can walk as I do. It is a point we try to make in the teaching of dissimilar reasoning. It is the way to acquire individuality, though often at the cost of some other factors which are important. That is why every Man is graduated into the world. Generally, only those are brought back into the Organization who succeed in regaining those factors dropped earlier. Experience can be your only teacher, and the final examination must take place in your own mind, under the supervision of your own sensibilities. When you have made proper recovery of the values I refer to, you will know it—and I will know it. Recovery is self-evident, allowing of no further question.

"You will then be in readiness for further service to the Organization . . . perhaps among the Searchers, as your father was, or in some other equally important phase of our activities.

"Meanwhile, you will be in good hands. We will have an opportunity to look further into the unique qualities of your divisible mind through various laboratory experiments. You will not see me often, as I must spend much of my time at the Institute. And now . . ." He stood up, offered Kor his hand. "Goodbye, my boy, and good luck to you!"

Disappointed, Kor allowed himself to be ushered out.


## 14.   DUTY—AND LOVE

The study of the unprecedented phenomenon of Kor Danay's divisible mind progressed slowly. A laborious molecule-count of the brain structure yielded no clue. Nor could he explain the divisibility which he made use of at will.

"Apparently," he suggested, "the divisible function of the mind bears the same relationship to ordinary superconscious functioning that the latter bears to the normal use of mind among untrained human beings. It seems likely that a regimen of training might also produce the ability to use the divisible function."

Dr. Han shook his head, pointed to the wavering chart of Kor's electropsychograph.

"Our modern methods," he said, "are refined to the highest degree. Out instruments can detect the barest, most latent superconscious potentiality. Not all minds, you know, can be trained to full use of the superconsciousness. That ability seems to be evidence of a mutational quality in the individual. Perhaps it occasionally flashed out as a symptom of 'genius.' What you have may be a further mutation of the mutation. If so, there may be others with the same ability. On the other hand, you may be the only one."

Slowly, Kor Danay grew to realize that he was unique. It made him at least moderately content with his lot as a temporary guinea pig of the Scarlet Sage psycho-scientists. He passed months in their company, in the performance of laboratory experiments.

During that time, he saw a lot of Soma, too. After her work period was done, and Kor's day at the laboratory was ended, they enjoyed the pleasures of the cavern-city together. The cavern was located a mile below the surface, about a hundred miles from Den-ver and the Institute near that city.

Sub-den was self-subsisting. A city of power, Sub-den was a stronghold of the physical strength of the Men, a power rivaling that of the Trisz, but a power that could not be used against the enemy.

In addition to his laboratory sessions, Kor attended scores of indoctrination lectures with groups of interested students.

"All the strength we can muster," lectured a gray-haired Man, "means nothing against the impervious armor of the Trisz. What is that armor? It is nothing we can see, nothing we can destroy. The subtle physical nature of the Trisz is beyond our power to harm."

Kor began to grow irked by his enforced sessions at the lab, sessions productive of nothing but puzzled frowns and much head-scratching. He wanted to be out and away, to attack the problem with action instead of dry lectures and random probing.

He sat with Soma at a table in the Pavilion of Dance. Cool, scented air wafted past them as the dancers circled in the blaze of a spotlight. Overhead, a simulated night sky blazed with stars in exact reproduction of the galaxy. A quartering moon progressed slowly across the artificial sky in time with the real moon that would have been visible outside.

"I don't know!" he said suddenly, holding his head in a paroxysm of despair. He slumped on his bent arms. "Soma! This is prison! How much longer will it go on? After all these months, the psychs have found out nothing except what I have been able to tell or show them. So what if my mind is a superior development of the normal mind? I can take only so much of this poking and prodding."

Soma touched his hand gently. He looked up into her face. "Please, Kor! What we are doing is just as important to the Men as the things others are accomplishing elsewhere."

"A year ago we talked with Val Shan!" he exclaimed. "I haven't seen him since that time. Twice I have tried and both times he was not available. They admit they've got something special in me. Why don't they use it?"

"They will, Kor. They will. Just wait."

"Wait! Soma, I have been extrapolating. I can't call up a single clear picture as most of the others can. I get a feeling from it that something wonderful is going to happen, but I don't know when! It's not knowing that is getting to be unbearable."

She squeezed his hand.

Kor looked at her askance. "I know. You would have me wait—wait! Well, I *have* been waiting! You know the story of my father—how I've dreamed all my life of joining the Searchers. If anyone can find out where the Trisz come from, *I* can! And I've told you how I can hurl the Fire. I am the only one who can do it, Soma. It takes *my* mind to do it. Nobody else can even be trained to do it."

She closed her eyes. "Please forget it for now, Kor, and let us enjoy the show. Perhaps soon the time will come."

"Soon—bah!" he growled.

She snatched her hand away from his. "I'm sick of it, Kor!" she snapped. "All you can think of is going away, out to the very edge of the Universe! Haven't you considered how I would feel about it?"

His expression slowly lost its exalted look. "Soma, you're crying!"

"Your mighty mind!" she blazed at him in sudden fury. "That's all you think of! A hundred generations of Men have fought the Trisz in silence, without glory. And what have *you* to say for it all? *You* can whip the Universe all by yourself, but you can't do one little thing about me!"

She jumped to her feet, eyes blazing through her tears.

"I've had enough, *Sir* Kor! Go tell Val Shan how mighty you are! Perhaps he hasn't found it out yet."

Soma had reached the lighted street in a precipitate rush before Kor caught up with her. She shook his placating hand from her arm, kept her head held high and avoided looking at him.

"Soma! Please don't run! Stop now . . ."

Her face was grim, tear-streaked.

"All right, I've stopped. Now what?"

He caught and held her, oblivious of the passing crowd that eyed them with amused understanding.

Kor looked around. "Let's get out of this public place! I —I have something to say to you."

In the center of the cavern city was a large park. Everything grew in it from shrubs to pines. An artificial breeze swept through it now, rustling the foliage, whispering among the pine needles. They came out upon a small lake, ruffled and reflecting the glow of the artificial moon in the sky. There were many about on the dimly lit paths, but he finally found a bench fronting the lake. He drew Soma down beside him. He did not let go of her hands.

"If I had not stopped you, you would have kept on going, wouldn't you?"

She looked away, across the dancing wavelets of the artificial lake.

Kor said lamely, "Well, when you left me like that, it—it all came home to me. I was so interested in being a Man, I —well, I forgot what it is to be human, too!"

She leaned expectantly toward him. Kor caught her face suddenly between his palms and kissed her. She did not draw away. The tiny sigh she uttered could never have been called a cry of victory, but it served the same purpose.

"Soma, as long as we both have to stay here, we could— why, we could—!"

She frowned, then burst out laughing at his suddenly crestfallen look. "We could what, Kor?"

"Please marry me, Soma!" Kor breathed with sudden exultation.

"I never, never would have expected it, darling! When shall it be? It could be next Lodge day, of course."

"Certainly it would take you more than three days to get everything you need."

"I have everything already, Kor!" She beamed happily.

"I—I've been getting them together for months! I've spent nearly all my salary . . . !"

Kor sat back and eyed her with mock astonishment. "You knew I was under an oath of chastity, didn't you?"

"Oh, that. It expired forty-seven days ago. I've been keeping track, you see."

Val Shan was pleased with the arrangement.

He said, "I have been hoping for some thing like this, Kor. I am rather inclined to go along with the theory that your divisible type of mind represents a mutational element. It is possible that it can be passed on to future generations."

"That thought didn't occur to me," Kor replied.

"It wouldn't," smiled Val Shan. "If the future of the race were left to the conscious considerations of the individuals concerned, I'm afraid the race would have ceased to have a future long ago. That is why I have called you in for a talk, Kor."

Kor remained politely attentive.

"It appears to me that you have changed a great deal since you first came to Sub-den. It will not be necessary to keep you here much longer."

"The Searchers!"

Val Shan shook his head. "Not yet, Kor. Perhaps never, now that you are undertaking the obligations of family life. I have something else in mind equally interesting and active. As soon as you are married, come and see me again. I have a honeymoon planned for you."

Kor looked blank. "What is a—what did you call it?"

Val Shan laughed. "A honeymoon is an ancient expression signifying travel by newlyweds. A journey all alone. You will understand its meaning"—he paused to smile slowly—"before the trip is over."

The ceremony did not take place the following Lodge day. There was too much to be done, in spite of Soma's preparations. Getting married was a more intricate process than Kor had thought . . . or Soma, either. It was two Lodge days later before all was in readiness.

No amount of training could have prepared Kor for this. Fortunately, his active participation was not necessary. He followed where Soma led and others, including Sir Ten Roga, whom Soma was overjoyed to find still alive, pushed him. Like bridegrooms since the beginning of time, he merely stood on his feet, did as he was told.

## 15. THE TRAGEDY OF LAREL IV

"Have you heard of the Colonization Survey?" Val Shan wanted to know. The term was a vague one to Kor Danay. All his research had been concerned with the activities of the Search Battalions.

"Do you mean searching for the human colonies planted by the Trisz?"

"No. That is part of the Search Battalion work. We have another activity, which is listed as the Colonization Survey. When the time comes to remove the People from Earth, we intend to scatter them as widely as possible, colonizing the younger worlds throughout space. However, before the People can be moved to any of these worlds, a lot of field work must be done."

The older man's words filtered through Kor's shroud of disappointment. But this, at least, was freedom. He would be able to leave Sub-den.

"I plan to send you out as a field researcher," Val Shan went on smoothly. "What you will be required to do is make a detailed analysis of living possibilities on all the worlds of which a list will be supplied to you. Your first sortie will take perhaps a year."

"A year!" Kor sat upright. "But, Sir—"

"You are thinking of Soma. So am I. You may take your wife with you."

"But she can't—"

"No, she can't teleport herself as you or I could, Kor. Therefore, you will have to teleport her, along with an analytical laboratory. A spaceship, in effect."

Val Shan stepped to the wall of his office and pressed an invisible stud. The room lights dimmed almost to extinction as the wall slowly parted to disclose a dazzling vista. Countless stars blazed before Kor's eyes as if he floated free in space, far from any sun.

"Out here, at the edge of the galaxy," said Val Shan, "there is a host of young worlds, many of which have never been touched by the Trisz. They are perfect worlds—much the way Earth was a million years ago, perhaps. They have sunny, equable climates, an abundance of moisture and vegetation. Some are sparsely inhabited, others have no inhabitants other than primitive types of animals and plants. The analytical laboratory is complete with equipment for recording the ecological data you will be required to gather."

A plastic bubble floated in the stratosphere of the planet Larel IV. It gleamed like a droplet of mercury against the blue-black sky in which brighter stars shot gleaming pencils of light. The GO-type sun of this system, a yellow dwarf as Earth's sun had once been, blazed at a distance of 112,000,000 miles from the planet. The bubble dropped slowly toward the cloud-wreathed face of Larel IV, a sparkling mote in the immensity of the upper air.

Soma was in an ecstasy of excitement at the view-port. "Look, Kor, how thick the air is! You can hardly see the surface at all. It's all blue and stringy looking . . . Will we be able to breathe it?"

Kor's mind automatically controlled the descending bubble. Strange fields of force bathed every molecule of the vessel and its occupants, held them hovering in defiance of gravity, or permitted them to move in whatever direction he willed.

"That is the effect of water vapor in the air," he told her aside. "Those fluffy bits and the strings are clouds of water droplets. Under certain conditions, the droplets condense and fall as rain. Have you ever seen rain?"

She looked at him, round-eyed. "I've heard of rain at some places on Earth, but it has never rained at Ka-si since I can remember."

"You will see plenty of it here," Kor laughed.

He jockeyed the vessel down to an altitude of only a few thousand feet and hovered over the white-capped, dark blue expanse of a heaving sea. The bubble drifted on the wings of a swift sea-wind.

Larel IV was an Earth-type planet of slightly larger diameter than Earth itself, but the pull of gravity at the surface was only negligibly greater. Kor checked through the original Searcher report. The planet possessed plains, jungles, and mountainous areas that swarmed with wild animals. The human-type indigents consisted of a few widely separated tribes of cave-dwellers, probably in the dawn of Stone-Age culture.

The plastic bubble drifted with gathering speed over feathering whitecaps far below.

"We might spend a month here, or longer," he decided.

"We can take as long as we please, and I, for one, am in no hurry! I am beginning to understand what Val Shan meant by that word—honeymoon!" He caught Soma to him and held her close.

The bubble drifted over a creamy coastline. A few small islands dotted the blue-black seascape a few miles from shore, surf-ringed, glinting in the yellowish glow of this alien sun.

"There is a river," Kor pointed out.

The river cut almost a straight streak through the lush savannahs bordering it. Its mouth broadened where it met the sea, fanning out in a surf-edged splotch of muddy water.

"We may as well start our investigation by following it to its source. A river like this would be a useful means of transportation for future colonies."

Quickly, Kor adjusted the recording equipment. An automatic camera began to whir and click. The analyzing laboratory gained speed and fled upstream.

The river branched and branched again, and they followed each time the larger of the branches. They passed over rough, broken country where the river hurled a high, plumelike cataract in a tumultuous fury of boiling spray from the thousand-foot-high lip of a precipice. They had reached the highlands, and ahead a range of mountains toothed the horizon.

Kor again checked his records against planetary latitude and longitude. It was somewhere in this region that the Searchers had originally located the tribes of manlike inhabitants who dwelt in caves and roamed the plains on hunting forays.

"What a beautiful world this is!" Soma cried, looking down. "Kor, I would like to live on a world like this."

Kor himself was possessed by the scene. A silver thread wound across the prairie, meandered among groves of trees, a sparkling stream sometimes hidden in dense foliage of the forest-clumps, sometimes half-visible when a light breeze momentarily shifted the leafy coverage. To westward, the mountains bulked, snow-covered and glistening against the eye-delighting blue of the sky, their great feet hidden in the blue mist of distance.

"We could land here," he said. He took Soma again in his arms and kissed her. "There will be lots of other worlds, you know. We have the Universe to choose from. And wherever you like it best, dearest."

Soma sighed happily.

The light in the miniature forest suddenly dimmed, became greenish-hued, casting a weird pallor over their skins. Soma gave Kor a startled glance.

"Kor, what's happening to the sun?"

Kor laughed. "Listen!" he said.

The hull resounded with a musical, rhythmic patter that grew louder and louder until it was a swishing roar. Soma put her hands over her ears. "What—what is it?"

"Rain, darling!"

"Rain? Is that what rain sounds like?"

"That's what rain sounds like on Larel VI. I put us down at the edge of a shower for your especial benefit! How do you like it?"

Soma ran to the view-port and peered out, but the view was obscured by a cataract of foaming water that gushed across the transparent panel.

"Rain . . . *rain!* Kor—let's go out in it!"

"We'd get wet!"

"I know it. Wouldn't it be wonderful? Water falling from the sky! More water than I ever saw before!"

He was checking the analyzers, determining the pressure and constituency of the Larelian atmosphere.

"Pressure slightly greater than Earth's oxygen, thirty per cent by volume, the remainder nitrogen and a few of the trace gases. Its breathable . . . and safe to go out, darling. But watch your footing."

The lock mechanism throbbed, and the door opened with a slight hiss as outside pressure entered the bubble. The door of the lock swung completely open and a wet spray of clean air and water vapor gushed inward.

Together, they dashed from the bubble, thrilling to the clean, wet feel of the drops splashing on their heads and hands. The forest around them smelled of growing things, of sodden humus, of life-giving moisture. The rain was warm, and it fell now in large, splattering drops. In a moment, both were drenched to the skin, laughing gleefully at the intimate caress of water upon their bodies.

Soma skipped playfully away, blithely dancing in the rain, through the underbrush, over fallen logs, laughing, caroling, enticing him on.

Kor knew what possessed her. It was the slight excess of oxygen in the atmosphere; that and the excitement of the rain and this strange new world. He called out to her to come back, but she laughed, waved, and skipped on.

As abruptly as it had begun, the rain stopped. The overcast broke. Clouds scurried like a herd of frightened, woolly sheep toward the horizon. The sun came out yellowbright and strong. Steam rose from the prairie. Soma collapsed among the suddenly stilled grasses.

He carried her back to the bubble. She was utterly exhausted, but she still laughed with an overflow of merriment that softened Kor's attempt at sternness.

"This isn't Earth, you know," he chided her. "You just can't exert yourself like that until you get used to the place!"

The following days were a heaven of delight for Soma. Kor worked assiduously with the analyzing and recording equipment, but there was still plenty of time left for play, for exploratory walks, for swimming and lying in the sun on the sandy bank of the creek. Many times, while he worked in the bubble, Soma went out alone. Whatever inhabitants this planet had, they assumed the status of mere animals in her mind, unreal and faraway. The world was theirs to enjoy as they pleased.

Kor had spent the day classifying a dozen varieties of stoloniferous prairie grasses and several others that might prove to be cereal- or grain-bearing. The latter were carefully filed in the hydroponics section of the bubble for further study under growing conditions. He made a last check of the instruments. Air and soil analyses were completed. The tapes held a complete record of plant cellular structure, as well as of a few small rodents that roamed the fields and woods. He had recorded about all that was worth while in this region. They would move on next to the mountains, then see what lay beyond. Kor went out into the living quarters to warn Soma that they were about to leave.

The airlock door was open to a sunny afternoon. A small, winged insect hummed busily just at the edge of yellow sunlight. Soma was not around, but he saw that she had left a note.

*Darling. Didn't want to disturb you—know we're about to leave, so have gone to the creek for one last bath. Join me? S.*

Kor smiled. Someday, he thought, he would see to it that she had a creek of her very own. Somewhere, they'd find the ideal world and settle down. Perhaps Larel IV was the world and this one was the creek.

He ducked out of the bubble and strode smartly along the path they had worn to the creek. He could hear Soma splashing in the water, singing melodiously in sheer exuberance of living.

Kor came out of the underbrush upon the bank of the creek—and froze.

He apprehended the entire, kaleidoscopic scene with one swift sweep of his mind—the purling, musical water, blue in the open reach of its bend, dull green in the shade of its banks. It mirrored leaves that fluttered on bending boughs, mossy-flanked boulders; and Soma, reflected in broken arcs upon the rippled pool; and above her a something half-seen, a thing of horror that rippled almost invisibly upon the air as it came down silently, remorselessly, and enveloped the girl.

*Trisz!*

The hateful thought cut like a knife across Kor Danay's mind. He stood bemused, watching as if fascinated. What was the Trisz doing? As the invisible vibrations of the Trisz enveloped her, Soma appeared hazy and distorted in outline, her head thrown back, arms outflung, back arched.

For an instant, Kor struggled within himself. He might have flung the full power of his mind at that alien thing to save the life of his beloved, but a lifetime of training pulled the other way. A monstrous hammer began to beat upon a clanging anvil in his brain, each blow a metallic clangor of words that leaped upon him: *I do most solemnly vow . . . the invulnerable Trisz . . . can't use your power . . . don't . . . it's killing her . . . don't . . .*

Desperately he fought to overthrow the discipline of a lifetime. And failed. The force of habit was too strong for sudden overthrow.

The instant struggle rived his mind, shattered his consciousness. The instant he might have acted passed. Kor fell senseless; the monster fed, and passed on.


# 16. THE THURB


Night came down across the grassy plain and upon the singing stream. The stars stood out in all their blazing glory. Alien constellations wheeled across the foreign sky, dimmed behind a driving cloud, and vanished. Dawn brought with it a chill drizzle.

Kor Danay awoke. He looked at the rain-dimpled creek and saw that it was water, but his comprehension went no further. The bubble lay behind him, but he had no memory of the laboratory, of its purpose, of whence it had come, nor of the passengers it had carried.

One other thought, a dim one, tugged at his mind. He was going to the mountains. What was there in the mountains that called to him? He did not know. He responded to the voiceless urge that welled from his subconscious. Where else was there to go, save to the mountains?

Of how many times the sun rose on his wanderings, Kor had no remembrance. He did not pause to eat. A part of his superconsciousness functioned automatically, drawing sustenance from the sub-levels of consciousness, restoring and rebuilding his body as he wore it out in his ceaseless trek. An ordinary human being would have died under these conditions. His body was caked with dried mud. His beard had begun to grow heavily.

Weeks passed. Vaguely, Kor became aware that he followed a swale that led gradually upward. The ground was rocky in places and the grass was short and tufted. Conifers whispered in the breeze; ripening cones hung like shuttered lanterns upon wind-lifted boughs. He had reached the tumbled region of the foothills.

A pair of feral eyes glared lambent yellow upon the Man's progress. The *kther* twitched its long tail, ran a pink tongue over fanged jaws. The beast lifted its horned head over the bulwark of rock behind which it crouched, then slid its cat-like body gracefully over and down the slope.

The swale flattened, widened into a grassy meadow. Deer streamed out of its far end, running for the safety of the forested slope above. They had caught the scent of the creeping *kther*, intent upon its prey.

Kor did not pause in his stride, nor cast a glance behind. The animal launched itself from the rock, bounded after its prey. At a dozen yards' distance, it halted, forepaw uplifted, and yowled hatefully.

Slowly, the Man turned. He saw the beast, behind it a stretch of grassy meadow giving upon the rocks that hemmed this cuplike depression. His mind stirred with a sluggish curiosity and he took a step toward it.

Other eyes watched the two—six pairs of brown orbs hidden in deep sockets, shadowed by bushy brows. A hunting party of thurbs had come over the ridge in search of the deer wont to frequent this grassy park. They stood transfixed at sight of the Man and the savage *kther* facing each other.

"That one is not a thurb," spoke An-Ga, leader of the hunters and chief of the tribe of Go. "Look at the color of him . . . and see the hair upon his head and face! Can he be human?"

"Whatever he is," said Strob, the chief's brother, "he has no fear. See—he advances upon the *kther!*"

"He will be torn to pieces!"

"The *kther* is the deadliest of beasts!"

"What can he do against a *kther?* He has no weapon!"

Two yards apart, the Man and the snarling *kther* faced each other, the Man curious and wondering. The *kther's* jet fur stood erect along its weaving spine, down which ripples ran to the long, twitching tail. Great yellow eyes peered unblinking at the Man. The red mouth opened in a soundless snarl.

Kor stopped, puzzled by the creature's manner. While he pondered the problem, the *kther* drew itself into a quivering heap, bunched its limbs; then, with all the power of steely muscles, it sprang.

He observed its rearing assault with indifference. The need to kill had not yet occurred to him. The great bulk seemed to cover the intervening space in a slow, flowing motion . . . then the *kther* crashed down upon him. Flashing claws ripped like scimitars. Scalding pain gushed over Kor's back and flanks. He willed the beast to die . . . and the power of his mind lashed out of its thrall of darkness.

The great *kther* squalled and rolled kicking on the grass.

Painfully, Kor dragged himself to his feet. He stood swaying, and stared at the *kther*. The great beast was dead. Kor felt faint. He toppled over, measured his length on the grass.

Awe-struck, the thurb hunters peered from their rock cover.

"Indeed," cried An-Ga in a tremendous voice, "he is no thurb, but a Great One!"

"But a Great One!" cried his little band of followers.

"Let us go to the Great One. Perhaps he needs our help!"

Skin-clad, trailing spears, the bald-headed thurb rushed into the meadow, gathered around conqueror and conquered.

"He still lives," announced An-Ga, feeling Kor's body. "But he is wounded. The *kther* ripped him with its claws."

"*Aie!* He will die, then! Whom the mighty *kther* whips with his claws goes down into the world of shadows!"

"Unless he is a Great One!"

A hoarse exclamation broke from a bending thurb.

"Look—his wounds! The Great One heals himself!"

The hunters bent, staring with eyes big and round. Slowly, the gaping wounds in Kor's flesh were closing, knitting, healing of themselves. As they watched, the last furrow closed itself, and the Sage lay without a scratch to mar his skin.

The thurb began to shout. They shook their spears and danced around and around Kor and the fallen *kther,* trampling flat the lush grass, chanting with wild, primitive joy.

"Hail the Great One! He has vanquished the *kther!* He has healed his wounds! Hail the Great One! *Aie—!*"

On and on, the thurb danced and yelled, their minds intoxicated by what they had witnessed.

Kor Danay rolled over and sat up. The din was deafening. He had no memory of combat with the *kther*. He looked at its body without interest, swung his gaze to include the yelling thurb. They saw his look, broke and ran. Kor sat and resumed contemplation of the *kther*. He wondered what it was and why it did not move.

At last he got to his feet, stretched lazily, and began to stride rapidly toward the head of the meadow and the forest that lay beyond.

The thurb grouped themselves in silence, watching him go.

"The Great One!" cried Strob. "He is leaving us!"

"Catch him!" ordered An-Ga.

The thurb looked at him. Who was a fool among them? Was the stranger not a Great One? Had he not slain a *kther?* None ventured forward until all moved in a body, slowly. They crept after Kor, calling out, pleading, placating. Kor did not hear them; he reached the edge of the forest, sat down on the exposed root of a tall pine and looked back the way he had come.

An-Ga led the rest by half a spear's length, a position

forced upon him by virtue of his chieftainship. He croaked dismally, "Stay, O Great One!"

Kor stayed.

He began to wonder about the advancing thurb. They were manlike, heavily muscled, almost hulking in stature. They had wide, bushy eyebrows, but their heads and faces were hairless. Their bodies, where not covered by wolf-skins, were revealed as coarsely haired.

The thurb saw Kor looking at them and gathered in a knot to confer. Afterward, An-Ga turned from his fellows, advanced a few paces and laid down his spear. Kneeling then, he backed away on his knees to rejoin the group. One by one, the others came forward, dropped their spears and retreated on their knees.

They began to chant, a meaningless jabber, but now Kor felt something in the depths of his mind which spoke for these simple people.

"We are thurb, O Great One! We lay our spears before thee."

The sense broke into meaningless gabble, became a dismal mouthing of sounds.

Kor got up and strolled toward the piled spears. He looked down at them. They were long shafts of wood, fitted with sharp points of stone.

"Take our spears, O Great One."

Once again, Kor caught the sense of the thought and looked toward the kneeling thurb. Something about them stirred him with pity.

*These are spears,* Kor thought. *These creatures are thurb. I am not a thurb. I am a Great One.*

He felt suddenly, strangely happy, as if he had solved an upsetting problem. He held up both hands and pronounced the only word he could remember: "Kor!"

"Kor—Kor!" cried the thurb together.

They leaped to their feet, babbled, waved their arms.

Kor Danay turned his back on them and stalked off into the forest. He forgot about them completely. The thurb followed him for three days, deeper and deeper into the forest. Their strength flagged. Their spears grew heavy to carry.

"He eats not, neither does he drink!" protested An-Ga. "And he stops but briefly to sleep! How can we keep up with him, we who have not eaten for three days?"

"Let us go," urged Strob. "We will return to our cache of meat by the meadow where we found the Great One. We will forget him, and hunt meat for our people on the plains."

"We have followed him for three days," returned An-Ga. "We are sick with hunger. We should starve before we got back to our cache."

"How long can a man go on without eating, Great One or not?"

"We must have food and water!"

"Why is this Great One important to us anyway? Why do we follow him?"

"Have not the old men of the tribe related that the Great Ones love the thurb? What love has this fellow shown for us?"

So they argued and harangued among themselves. Kor halted, beset by a baffling clamor of thoughts. The thoughts came from the thurb, and spoke of discontent, unhappiness, hunger and thirst. The thurb minds told him that hunger was suffering, but he did not know what suffering was, either. What is thirst? Thirst is suffering of a different sort, but similar to hunger. Kor fondled the thought, unconsciously molding it into the abstraction of need. Hunger and thirst were the expression of needs. One was for food and the other for water.

He turned to An-Ga and asked, "What is thirst?"

An-Ga said, "Lord, we need water and food. And rest, too, for the way has been hard, following you."

Kor grasped the thought. "Water?"

The word was not the same as the thurb word for it. An-Ga made motions of dipping cupped hands and lifting them to his lips.

He closed his eyes. There was a spring bubbling out of the mountainside barely a half mile away. He sensed its presence, seized An-Ga by the shoulder, faced him in the direction of the spring and shoved. An-Ga staggered a step forward and stopped. Kor reached to seize another thurb, but the fellow drew back.

Kor swung away from them, burst into a swinging lope down the mountainside. The pitiful band of thurb scrambled hastily after him. A few minutes later, they lay in contented relaxation, having drunk their fill.

*Food,* thought Kor. *Thurb need food.* He was at a loss to account for what food might be until a thurb conjured up an impression of a deerlike animal. He saw the thurb running through the forest, spear ready. He saw him stop, crouched, then the cast of the spear. A nimble-footed, antlered creature fell crashing to the forest floor. *Such is food,* thought Kor.

He sat down on an outcropping of rock by the bubbling spring and closed his eyes. His mind swept out, touched a family of squirrels eating pine nuts in a nearby tree. They had no antlers. They were not food. He thrust his mind farther afield.

A herd of the deerlike creatures grazed in a grassy meadow. Hunger had weakened the thurb. They were too weak to march so far. Kor continued to sit, uttering no sound. The deer lifted their heads, turned as if in response to a call. They began to drift toward the meadow's edge, faster and faster, until soon the herd streamed at top speed through the forest. Their dainty feet stamped the turf . . . faster . . . faster.

Strob said, "He has led us to water, but do we starve now? I hunger."

"He is a Great One," replied An-Ga. "Shall we ask after the ways of Great Ones? He has given us water. Be content. He will give us food."

The thurb huddled in a semicircle before Kor, clutching their spears. An-Ga's primitive ears twitched. Had that sound been the click of a hoof upon stone? He uttered a harsh command. The thurb melted away from Kor's lone, intent figure.

The deer came on, walking fast, eyes rolling, muzzles dewed. The thurb saved their wonder for later. Here was meat!

## 17.   THE GREAT ONE

The thurb were happy and contented, their faith restored in their Great One. Kor brooded in mystic silence. He accepted the thurb as his own. They were his people. They were why he had come to the mountains.

The thurb had struck fire from a flint spearhead and roasted part of their kill. They feasted and sang praises to Kor.

The thurb talked now of packing the rest of their meat and striking out in the morning for the cave that sheltered the tribe. Kor searched the thurb minds. He came away with a feeling of a hole among rocks, a cool place when the sun was hot, a warm place when wind and driven snow howled outside. There was something of shelter about a cave, something of comfort that had to do with fire, and something of something else, a feeling more than a fact. The word swam slowly into Kor's consciousness—home.

Home! Kor Danay felt an unexplainable ache. He was going home. He followed the meat-laden hunters as they struck off across the hogbacks.

Two days of hard packing over ridges brought them to a canyon with high, frowning escarpments of weathered rock. A snow-covered cone rose steeply above the canyon, smoke wreathing its crest. A small white cloud of water vapor condensed above the smoke and rained without end upon the unquenchable fires of the volcano.

The canyon floor leveled into a grassy sward. A spraying waterfall dashed in a broken cataract down the steep rocky side, pooled at the bottom and flowed in a sparkling stream southward. They came upon cultivated fields. Above the fields there were black holes in the canyon wall, topping a long slope of tumbled talus. Figures, tiny in the distance, jumped and gesticulated at the mouths of the caves. Faintly, shouts of welcome came to the ears of the returning hunters.

*Home,* thought Kor. He looked at the caves and the crowd of thurb. *Soma,* he thought, and he did not know why a sharp pain stabbed through his breast. He saw that An-Ga and the other hunters were laughing and shouting back at the welcoming throng. He was pleased for them and forgot his pain.

There was feasting in the caves that night. Kor sat on a high rock in front of the caves, looking into the bright heart of a fire. A deerskin robe given him by An-Ga dropped from his shoulders. A wolfskin lay across his knees. Someone had brought wild flowers and piled them at his feet. Every thurb in the tribe of Go knew that Kor was a Great One.

A woman approached him with a gourd filled with savory venison. She offered it to Kor, but he turned his head away.

Tharg squatted by the campfire, and eyed Kor with sullen jealousy. Tharg was a mighty thurb, heavily muscled, mightily thewed. "Who is he, that you call him Great One?" he grumbled to a campfire mate. "Do we not know that the

Great Ones made thurb after their own likeness? What thurb is so hideously haired as he?"

Tharg's companion stopped gnawing at his portion of venison. "Not so hideous in the eyes of Tharg's mate, is he?"

Tharg growled and sprang erect. He scuttled across the intervening space and knocked his mate sprawling. Tharg stood then and glared at Kor, feet spread wide, toes gripping the ground, his arms hanging loosely. He growled his displeasure.

A stone axe hurtled through the air, glinting in the firelight, thumped into the giant's ribs. Tharg yelled, went down with a look of wild surprise, clutching his breast.

"Be taught," An-Ga said calmly, retrieving his axe, "not to profane the Great One's presence with violence. Take your mate to your cave. If she annoys the Great One again, I shall have her whipped for all to see. Go! I, An-Ga, have spoken."

They gave Kor a cave of his own, above all the others, by the cliff path that led to the forested plateau above. They carpeted its floor with scoured sand from the creek bed in the canyon and piled it with skins and lustrous furs for his comfort.

He took no food or water, and there was no need for a fire. Alone, he lived in his cave and brooded on the eternal mystery of his being.

The days grew shorter, and the golden light of autumn settled upon the canyon. The hunters went out and returned with meat, which the women prepared for winter use by boiling and drying in the sun. Sometimes Kor went with the hunters and brought them an abundance of game.

The cave which served the tribe as a storehouse was piled with dried meat. The harvest of grain and cereals was brought in from the fields. Nightly, the hunters danced around the fires. They made up songs as they danced, songs that honored and praised the Great One who had come to live with them.

The first frost arrived. In spite of the sun, shining low in the south now, there was a piercing chill in the air. The hunters stayed away longer now, and returned with less game.

One day a group of hunters returned about noon. They had no meat, though they returned heavy laden. Their burden was the body of Hrol, son of An-Ga.

The people of Go stood around the litter and uttered

their piercing shrieks of mourning. Kor heard the noise, the weeping, wailing, and lamentation that arose from clustered women and children.

He came out of his cave. The tribespeople howled a high-pitched dirge over the litter. Kor frowned. The thought was clear in his mind—*Hrol is dead*. Kor went down to where the hunters had dropped the litter at the foot of the talus. He picked his way down the rocky slope. An-Ga knelt at the side of his son. Hrol's mother lay upon the boy's breast, weeping.

Kor looked a question and read the answer in the mind of a returning hunter. Hrol had made a kill—an *url*—a small, three-toed creature that ran upon the plain with great speed. Only Hrol could have run to within spearing distance of the nimble *url*. Out of a clump of cane sprang a vicious *kther*, razorlike claws ripping at the thurb. Forgetting their fear of the *kther* in the face of peril to their beloved Hrol, the hunters had rushed forward and speared the beast. But Hrol was clawed to death by the mighty beast.

Kor knelt, seized the mother by her skin robe and tossed her aside. Somewhere in the back of his mind, he was conscious of a universe of spinning electrons that darted and danced as tiny motes of supernal light. He stood up at last, gestured to An-Ga to go away. The chief crept back from the litter, head bowed. The tribespeople grew tense and hushed.

He held out his hands, looked first at one, then at the other. He turned them palms down over the body of Hrol. Something like a soundless sigh passed through his mind. Strange words murmured just over the horizon of his consciousness. He could barely make them out . . . *desire is our scourge . . . need is our blessing . . . resolve is our armor . . . will is our weapon . . .*

Where these words came from, Kor did not know. He was conscious that they flowed like music through his mind, that the dancing electrons kept time with their cadence.

He said, "Hrol—get up!"

Hrol stretched, yawned, blinked his eyes. He regarded the fascinated onlookers with puzzlement. He rolled over on the litter, rested on his elbow.

"The *url* is mine!" he growled. "Where is it?"

He got up from the litter, swinging his arms and flexing his muscles. He did not look at Kor. Hrol's mother threw herself upon him, screaming with joy. An-Ga seized his son's hand. Tears streamed from his eyes. The tribespeople crowded around, crying out with joy.

Kor Danay looked at them, sensed their emotion. He turned and went back to his cave. No one saw him go.

The skies turned from sunny to gray, and a thin spindrift of snow whipped through the canyon on the teeth of a bitter wind. The top of the smoking cone was hidden in the cloud cover; trailing mists hid its snowy flanks. The conifers had long ago dropped their cones, and the grass in the canyon was withered and brown. The hunters had given up the chase and spent their time huddled now over fires in the caves.

One morning, An-Ga brought a thurb girl into Kor's cave. She was young and comely. An-Ga spoke, but it was difficult for Kor to make out more than part of what he was saying. He gathered that the girl was Eldra, a gift of the tribe to be woman and servant to him.

"She is the youngest born of my brother Strob," An-Ga said gravely. "Of my own flesh and blood."

"I need no servant," Kor said. "Go. Return to your people."

Eldra could not understand his tongue.

"Go."

The girl went and Kor resumed his position of meditation. Outside, a woman screamed. The noise irritated him; he got up and went to the cave mouth to look out.

A few yards away, An-Ga held the screaming Eldra doubled over, her head held forcibly atop a boulder. Beyond An-Ga stood her father, Strob, balancing a huge rock in upthrust hands. The muscles in his arms and shoulders were knotted with strain. As Kor looked out, Strub hurled the stone downward upon his daughter's head.

Something slipped in Kor's mind. The boulder slammed sideways and splintered into fragments against the rocky wall of the canyon. An-Ga and Strob looked surprised, then fell on their faces.

"We would have punished her, that she displeased our lord. Forgiveness . . ."

Kor pointed to the caves of the thurb. Ashamed, the two got to their feet and slunk away. Eldra had stopped screaming. She lay with eyes closed. Kor picked her up and carried her into his cave. He dropped her rudely on the floor and her eyes flew open. She got up, rubbing herself where the drop had bumped her. He sat down in his pose of meditation and forgot all about Eldra.

Eldra was happy to share the cave with Kor. She kept the fire burning at the cave mouth during the long winter nights and the short, bitter days. She asked no help of the tribe and received none. And when she cooked her meals and ate alone, a great wonder grew in her that the Great One required no food.

While he slept by night, she would sit in the cave mouth, by the tiny fire she kept going to frighten away wild beasts. She would listen to the howl of the wind and the lash of snow, and she grew warm inside with the thought that she was guardian of the sleeping Great One. On clear, starry nights, she peered into the mystery of space and wondered what the tiny lights were. She thought perhaps the Great One could tell her, if only he could speak the language of the thurb. She could teach him, she thought. Why not? Besides, there was something she had to tell him for which signs were not sufficient.

## 18.   THE INVADERS

Eldra was a model of efficiency at cave-keeping. She kept their quarters clean, was alert to every move that Kor made. During the long evenings, she fed the fire and talked to him, sang to him, until gradually her words began to have meaning for him. He was learning the simple language of the people of Go.

There was sickness among the tribe that winter, and Kor healed them. When food ran low, he lured a great, slow-moving, fur-covered beast into the canyon for the hunters to slay.

When the last snows melted in the spring, Eldra was already big with child. Kor Danay left his cave and went up the rocky path to the forested plateau above. He had found a pleasant glade there, bright with the first blossoms of spring. In it, he would sit for hours and meditate in silence.

His conversations with Eldra during the winter had tapped the hidden store of his memory, but no piece could be fitted to another to make sense. Who was Soma?

He dreamed of a lovely face with sparkling, sea-green

eyes. He stared at the ground, seeing her there in his mind's eye. Electrons streamed in whorls of ecstasy through his consciousness. Bright motes of sparkling luminescence swirled around him in the glade, glinted against the background of somber conifers, of leafing underbrush. The swarms of brilliant sparkles cascaded between his palms, a leaping torrent of living flame, and disappeared into a shapeless bulk that seemed to grow on the turf at his feet. At last the sparkling motes dimmed and died. Kor looked at what he had wrought. She was Soma! From somewhere, his nighted memory had dredged up the matrix for her creation. A sob caught in his throat.

"Soma!"

She did not move. He touched her. The flesh was cold.

Kor wept. He destroyed the image and built again. He could not make her live. Each time he tried, Soma's body returned as preciously perfect as the dream that inspired her. Each time she was dead, and Kor destroyed her.

It was two months before Eldra's time. In spite of her bulk, she remained furiously active while Kor retired to his glade to create. With greater practice, a facility came into his handling of the creative matrix. He sat in a mist of electrons, molding, shaping, trying desperately to capture the elusive pattern that would bring his creation to life. A buzzing voice cut across his mental horizon.

"What are you doing, creature?"

"Go away," said Kor.

"What are you, creature?"

"I am a Great One," replied Kor. "Can you not see I am creating?"

He looked up. The glade was empty except for himself. His glance came back to a wavering patch between two trees . . . a shimmering spindle of disturbed air that gave him a qualm. Almost, he was afraid.

"I do not read your voice, creature," returned the buzzing thought-note.

The buzz was in his mind rather than his ears. It was reedy, high-pitched, and brought with it a nervous pseudomemory that made him tremble. The cloud of sparkling electrons hovering around him winked out. Automatically, without conscious thought, Kor touched his knee, his chin. His fingers made signs.

"You speak the sign language of the Trisz," said the voice. "What are you doing here?"

He signed a reply, his hands responding to the subconscious pattern of his thought.

"I am a Great One. Begone, lest I destroy you!"

The Trisz swayed nervously at the edge of the glade. Kor felt a sense of alarm. He had no desire to argue with it. He drew his mind back into the confines of his skull, sat stolidly silent.

He did not hear the child break from the underbrush at the lip of the precipice and run toward him across the glade. The Trisz darted instantaneously. It was a flashing blur that whipped across the grassy space, enveloped the child.

"If you are a Great One," it mocked, "save this child!"

The thurb child stiffened in the vibratory grip of the Trisz, on its face an expression of frozen horror.

A glare of light burst in Kor's mind. He reacted automatically, with powers he did not know he posseseed. He whipped the glade into time-stasis. The lashing field enveloped the Triz. For an instant, his mind was dazzled with a flood of perception from the Trisz. His mind went *through* space, penetrated time. The Trisz shrilled its mental agony and ceased to exist. The flow of thought ceased abruptly, sank beneath the fogs that clouded Kor's mind. The thurb child ran screaming back the way it had come.

Kor sat and pondered what had happened. He was deeply shaken, but he did not know why. He did not know what he had done to the alien thing. He only knew that he had felt the urge to destroy, and this something that was on his mind, on the other side of the veil, had burst forth and retreated . . . and the Trisz was destroyed.

He listened. Shrill cries drifted faintly upward from the caves below. They bore a sound of alarm, fear and anger. He stood up as Eldra burst heavily from the head of the path and stumbled toward him.

"Lord, Lord, save us! The Great Ones from the sky are come!"

Kor seized her and shook her. She was hysterical with fright. A score of tribespeople burst shouting from the head of the path.

"Great ones from the sky steal the people of Go!"

Kor turned impatiently toward the path, but it erupted a hurrying horde of cave men.

He said, "Tell me about it—quickly!"

"They are like yourself, Lord, and like the thurb as well.
111

They walk in gleaming garments and a strange light accompanies them in the air as they go. They have torn caves out of the sky and brought them into the valley. They are putting the people of Go into their caves!"

He swung away, across the glade and into the wood. From the hogback, he would be able to see into the valley, where the canyon came out upon the broader, low-lying stretch among the foothills. He went swiftly, tearing through the underbrush. Like a pack of baying hounds, the thurb streamed after him, calling upon him for succor.

He stood on the lip of the precipice that overlooked the valley. The cliff towered above it a thousand feet or more. Three silvery, oval shapes hugged the green carpet of the valley floor. The ships of the Trisz shone in the sun, awakening feeble memories in Kor's darkened mind. He willed, and his supersenses lashed out in a widening circle, sensed the surroundings. A struggle took place in the caves. The cave people were fighting for their lives, but the invaders paralyzed them where they stood, carried them out through the gaping cave mouths.

Kor touched their minds. Creatures of the Trisz, these, taking the people of Go. He said to Eldra, "Kor's enemies, Eldra's enemies. Kor is angry with them for coming here."

Eldra wailed, cried out her lord's saying to the people.

"Slay the enemy, Lord!" cried the people of Go. "Protect us!"

Kor brooded solemnly over the scene below. Hatred screamed inside of him. The blue sky pressed close. The sun was a blazing shield in the sky. He poised his body as if to leap into the abyss—and abruptly vanished from the sight of the cave people. A moan of terror went up from the thurb.

On the surface of the distant sun, a mighty storm swirled. A suction of energy funneled into the passage hewed through subspace by the Sage's mind. Where he had stood, blazing luminescence shot tongues of fire. And suddenly, a stream lashed out. Scintillant flame poured roaring into the valley, and Kor stood again, rigid upon the lip of the precipice.

Already the thurb had begun to run in crazed fear. As the frightful surge of pure energy blasted into the valley, the ground shook under their feet. Thunder rolled deafeningly from mountain to mountain, set up crescendoing vibrations that made the pines whip, set the boulders to grinding underfoot. The land heaved and buckled.

A mist sprang up from the valley, a mist of deadly, radiating particles that hung in an opalescent pall over the crimson glow of destruction. The mountain heaved and shook again. The valley boiled with flame. A titanic roar as of all the thunderclaps that ever were slammed down from above. The mountain groaned and shook to its core.

A voice screamed, "The mountain! The Great One of the mountain throws fire!"

The volcano trembled, lurched. Flames shot from its simmering peak, coiled into the stratosphere. Dark, formless objects shot upward with a thunderous sound. Black, greasy smoke boiled from the shuddering cone, rolled down the snow-covered flank in which long black gashes had begun to show. Lightning flashed and quivered in a sky abruptly gone dark.

"Lord, Lord!" whimpered Eldra.

Kor seized her arm, hurried her ahead of him. The air was thick with smoke and hot, falling ash as they lurched down the path. Sometimes the ground shook so that it seemed they must be hurled on the rocks far below. Screams pierced the dark. Eldra clung to Kor, sobbing.

He fought his way grimly downward, booting the struggling tribespeople ahead of him. At the bottom, they would have run for the caves, but the cliff face was slowly disintegrating and falling in chunks. Cave men were running in all directions, among them figures dressed in the silvery space uniform of the Trisz. All were one in this inferno. The boiling smog of the volcano poured into the canyon, obliterating sight.

Kor began to shout at those who ran past. His mind reached out, and he cried to them to run up the canyon. Licking flames crept in from the valley, a blistering hell whose fires would rage unchecked for a millennium. Soon the magma from the erupting peak would be pouring into the canyon.

The cave men stormed up the canyon, over the hogback and into the ravine beyond. When it grew impossible to see more than a foot or two in any direction, Kor left off shouting. He could sense a few tribesmen still wandering dazed in the midnight of the canyon, but his voice could no longer be heard above the crash and roar of the bursting volcano. The ground shook and swayed, throwing Eldra flat with every other step.

He gathered her in his arms and set off swiftly up the canyon. He could move faster than the cave men. He did not need eyes to see where he was going. As he passed stumbling stragglers, he roared to them to make haste. The universe spun around him. He sensed a tremendous crack that suddenly opened in the solid ground ahead. Screams cut through the rancid smoke as a few blundered over the edge and plunged into the abyss.

Kor ran around the end of the crack, where the solid rock was split almost to the wall of the canyon. He ran as a deer runs, balancing himself precisely in spite of the darkness that blinded his sight. He carried his burden gently, easing the jar of his running with the springlike muscles of his arms. Eldra moaned softly in his grasp.

The larger part of the tribesmen were already pouring over the hogback. As he topped the rise, he found the air thinning slightly into a grayish, opaque mistiness. He followed the cave men over, under the swaying conifers, shouting as he went, urging them to scale the next ridge and the one beyond that, and to keep on going until the menace of the erupting volcano was left far behind.

All afternoon and all night long, the fleeing cave men blundered through the brush, scrambled down steep slopes, laboriously climbed the following ridges. When the ash no longer rained, when the fire bombs ceased to thud among them, they had reached the edge of the foothills and it was dawn. The sun rose on a weary, spent group that flung itself on the bank of a creek and drank greedily.

Far behind, Kor Danay struggled over a ridge with his burden. Eldra's arms were tight around his neck, and she screamed with every step he took. Her face was dewed with the cold sweat of agony. Kor knew what it meant. He laid Eldra on the ground, knelt beside her, tried to collect his confused sensibilities. He had healed the sick in the caves, he had banished the pain of the wounded. How had he done it? He laid his hands on the tossing woman, and she screamed at the contact.

Kor tried to collect his thoughts. He sought frantically for the sparkling, darting electrons, but none came. His power was gone. Shocked horror held him rigid, stricken with grief . . . and the baby was born dead. The life went out of Eldra, too, and Kor dropped his head in his hands and wept.

The sky was lurid over the mountains. The volcano exploded with a muffled, drumlike beat.

The world was a screaming cacophony of horror. A vision of Soma hovered in the Sage's dimming mind—of Eldra torn with agony.

Darkness swooped upon the plain. Gentle hands reached out of the air, touched Kor Danay's body. His bonds fell away. He floated free, without weight. . . .


## 19.  THE RETURN

"We got the whole story, of course," said Devon, Technical Director of the Psycho-Neural Institute on the planet Gramm.

He sat behind an enormous desk—a desk sized to its master, for Devon was an enormous man himself. He sat loosely, sprawled back in his chair, chewing the stub of a cigar. He took the stub out of his mouth, and waved it over the array of charts, graphs, and typewritten commentaries that littered his desk.

"You have taken a great load off my mind, Doctor," Val Shan said, relieved.

Devon shook his cigar at a distant ash tray. Ashes showered the litter on his desk.

"You need have no worry, Sir. Kor is doing unusually well, considering the severity of his condition. We understand it better now, of course, then we did two months ago when you first brought him in—the fundamental aspect of his case, that is. His mind is quite normal now. Here—take a look at this material."

Devon handed over a sheaf of papers. Val Shan read rapidly through. Finally he lifted his eyes, stared through the open window at the greenish-tinged sky of Gramm, among the Far Stars, an isolated planet where the Men had established an ecological experiment station.

"I feel it will be difficult for me to face the boy," he said slowly. "I am responsible for his condition—for the loss of his wife. A great shock to him."

"He is completely recovered from that shock," Devon returned easily. "Actually, he suffered two distinct shocks simultaneously: the loss of his wife and his conflict with his Oath as a Man. His normal desire was to attack the Trisz with whatever power he could command and so attempt to save the woman's life. Had he done this, he might have saved his mind. The conflict between his duty to his wife and his duty to his Manhood was too much for him to bear. Remember, the decision he had to make was a split-second one. His sanity shattered under the strain."

Val Shan weighed the papers in his hand. "He seemed to possess for a while an unconscious use of certain of his mental powers. Then he lost this use. How do you account for that?"

Devon shrugged. "You have said that his greatest drawback was personal pride; some of that would stick with him, below the conscious level. He went 'on automatic,' as we say. His powers burst forth automatically in response to some unusual call of his will.

"For the better part of a year, he went without food or water. The digestive and eliminative organs suffered especially—became atrophied. As far as his mind goes, Kor could be discharged today, but he needs a further period of physical acclimatization to return to the normal level.

"It is easy enough to speculate on why his powers deserted him entirely at the end. It probably was his subconscious realization that he had violated his Oath of Manhood in using his powers against the Trisz. He could not consciously reason this, of course. That's why the shut-off was so drastically final. Below the conscious level, he felt that he had degraded himself from the stature of a Man by violating his Oath. He was no longer worthy to be a Man."

"How long will you need to keep him here?"

"Six weeks, at least. Would you like to see Kor now, Sir?"

Kor Danay was relaxed in a deep leather chair. His hands were brown and emaciated. They rested moveless on the broad arms of his chair. He smiled, got up quickly as Devon entered with Val Shan.

"Sit down, sit down, boy!" Val Shan gestured violently and took Kor's hand as the latter sank back into his chair.

"I'll leave you, Sir. Lecture coming up," Devon said. "There are no restrictions on talking to the patient. When you are ready to leave, I'd like to see you again. Ask one of the nurses."

He smiled a friendly goodbye and left the two alone.

"I hope you like it here," Val Shan began awkwardly.

Kor nodded quickly. "They've been wonderful to me, Sir." His voice was swift, eager. He seemed buoyant with returned vigor.

"I am glad, Kor. I would like to say how sorry I am, but it seems rather useless. . . ."

Kor offered the ghost of a smile. "It really doesn't matter, Sir—too much. I brought it all on myself, of course. I —I'll tell you about that later. Just now, I'd like to say that I've made that—that recovery you told me I needed."

Val Shan nodded solemnly. "I told you that you would not need to mention it. I see that you have."

"If you don't mind, Sir, I want to talk about it. I—I thought there was something of professorial authoritarianism about you when you brought the subject up. I've learned you were right. You were referring to my pride, of course. Pride just does not go with being a Man. It's funny how proud you can be, and at the same time think you are the most humble creature in the galaxy! I'm grateful to doctor Naz for saving my memory of the Larelian episode. Without it, I should probably be pretty much the same old Kor. As it is, I can remember the height of my pride . . . when I thought I was a Great One. . . ." His lips twisted in a wry smile. "Better still, I remember the depths."

Val Shan smiled. "I thought you might like to know that we've kept an eye on the thurb. After your—disappearance, they migrated across the plain. They found the analyzing laboratory you landed there. Are you interested in hearing about it?"

Kor leaned forward. "Very much, Sir!"

"We had intended removing the laboratory, of course. We were searching for it and that is how we happened to chance upon the thurb. We made a mental survey of the situation and learned they had connected the bubble with you. They were happily settled around it—they called it the 'Sky Cave of the Great One, Kor.' I am afraid you are still a Great One to the thurb."

Kor shook his head wonderingly. "With the death of An-Ga, Tharg assumed a natural leadership. An-Ga would never have permitted it. The Go must have killed him."

"On the contrary, Tharg is very much alive. It seems that your chieftain's brother came out of the holocaust alive and assumed his brother's chieftainship. Tharg has a title under the new order. He is called Chief Steward of Kor!"

Kor mused on the strange turn-about of affairs among the thurb.

"That will all be changed, of course," he smiled, "when colonists are transported to the Larelian System."

"There will be no colonists on Larel IV. We have reserved it on our list as a very special kind of experiment."

Kor nodded. "You would arrange it that way. You took the bubble away, though, of course."

"Yes. We left them only their memories . . . to help them develop their minds. . . ."

Kor sighed. "Another thing I wanted to mention, Sir," he put in abruptly, "is that I had personal contact with the Trisz on Larel IV."

"I read that in Devon's report. Fortunately, the Trisz did not connect you with the destruction of their vessels. They attributed that to the volcano."

"Devon's report doesn't begin to state the situation, Sir. I found out everything there is to know about the Trisz!"

"What did you discover? Quickly, boy!"

"I—I'm growing very tired, Sir."

Val Shan stood nervously erect. "I shouldn't have tired you! I will go."

"It would be best, Sir."

Kor drew a folded paper from his pocket. "I understand I may not leave the hospital for a few weeks yet. I don't want to waste any time. I have made a list of a few things I should like to have brought to me here."

Val Shan scanned the list. "Electronic cybernograph— thousand kilo-volt energy pile, portable—silver wire—resistors—condensor-collectors. . . ." Val Shan's glance continued to the bottom of the impressive list. He snapped the paper crisply in his palm. "Is this important, Kor?"

"Extremely, Sir. Just a beginning, of course, to help me work out a few fundamentals. Later, I'll need a fully equipped psycho-physical laboratory and the mental resources of the entire Brotherhood of Men. But that stuff will do for the present."

Kor Danay faced his distinguished listeners in one of the large suite of rooms that had been turned over to his activities. Devon and Val Shan were there, and a company of about twenty of the keenest scientific minds in the Brotherhood of Men.

The curious machine at Kor's back half-filled the room. Looking at it, one had the impression of seeing only part of the machine—that it went on and on, into other spaces and other times.

"I want to begin my discussion," he told them, "with a

118

brief survey of the concepts underlying the work I have just accomplished here."

Devon drew a cigar from his pocket, focused his attention on the tip of it until the tobacco flamed, then settled back in his chair with a look of interest, blue coils of smoke wreathing his head. Val Shan and the others leaned forward.

"First, a brief recapitulation of the orders of reasoning. Deductive reasoning is our first order of rationalization. It is most highly exemplified in the field of mathematics. Mathematics, however, deals entirely with exact premises and exactness exists nowhere in our Universe. Mathematics, as a means of reasoning, therefore, can express only ideal conclusions.

"Inductive reasoning is the second order of rationalization. Isolated facts are brought together, and from their behavior, a general law is induced to explain them.

"Strangely enough, men thought for thousands of years that these two were the only possible methods of reasoning.

"In the early periods of our race, any mental or so-called psychic phenomenon not well understood was relegated to the supernatural category and ignored. What used to be called telepathy, teleportation, prevision, and so on, were considered by some to be supernatural manifestations. Others called them 'parapsychological phenomena.' Neither term is capable of semantic abstraction.

"Another inhibiting factor of the early discovery of third-order rationalization was the common misunderstanding held toward what then were variously labeled instinct, intuition, and the subconscious mind. Any mental phenonemon not yielding to empiric methods of investigation was either cast into one of the first two categories, or hastily dumped in the province of the third—and no attempt was made to define any of them.

"It was from these little known and largely discredited functions of the human mind that the first Men received what they thought to be hints of the existence of a third order of logic—that method of rationalization which transcends both deduction and induction and is the survival factor which works toward the preservation of the individual when all other methods of conscious reasoning fail. The form of third-order rationalization cannot be consciously detected as a function. The function is inferred by analyzing its results. Without the mental training to which the Men are subjected from early childhood, evidence of its existence is flighty and inconclusive—what used to be interpreted as instinct or intuition.

"On the other hand, the higher orders of third-order logic have never been exploded, even by the Men. Our attempt at extrapolation, for instance, is weak, hazy, and fraught with errors."

Kor laughed suddenly, explosively. "As a matter of fact, I myself committed the most colossal of blunders in trying to extrapolate—a blunder so important that it has rid our Universe of the Trisz, will completely change the future of the Men, and through them, of the People!"

Devon chewed heavily on his cold cigar and frowned with concentration. Val Shan appeared eagerly interested. "You said it *has* rid the Universe of the Trisz?"

Kor nodded. "Quite so. The Universe *has* been rid of the Trisz! Let us return to the planet Larel IV. Every act I performed there was plotted in advance. When I thought I was activating the third-order function to extrapolate future events, I actually sidestepped that function and made use of a *new* order of beyond-logic. Actually, what I did determined, rather than foretold, the future!"

Kor held up his hand. "I should be ashamed to say it," he grinned wryly, "but from the moment I left the Institute, instead of extrapolating the future, as I thought, I was determining the events of my own future through a system of determinant logic transcending the recognized third-order function. That is why my attempts at extrapolation failed—why yours failed, also." He nodded at Val Shan. "You could not foretell my future actions, because they had no relationship to past events. My every act was destined to bring me in the shortest possible time into intimate contact with the Trisz, so that I could learn the things which I have learned."

Devon stabbed with the odorous butt of his cigar.

"A blunder, as you put it, is easy to make in extrapolation. The perceived result may be only a figment of the imagination instead of a viridical picture of the future event. What gives you the impression that you were actually making the future?"

Kor waved a sheaf of papers aloft. "I have been working day and night with the cybernograph, integrating the factors. The cybernograph proves the assumption I made from observation—here is the math as well as the mechanics of the situation."

Val Shan and Devon both grabbed for the papers at once. Kor jerked them back. "This material will keep a while longer. The future has already been determined. The Trisz are already destroyed. Only I can change that chain of events, and I am not about to try!"

He frowned thoughtfully at his audience. "Back on Larel IV, there was an instant in which the Trisz mind was wide open to mine. I do not mean the mind of what you probably think of as that individual Trisz, but of *the* Trisz—the parent body, which does not exist in this space and time at all!"

Cries of astonishment went up from the assembly.

"The concept of contiguous universes, of probability universes, of interlocking universes, and so on, is not a new one." Kor gestured toward the machine at his back. "This device proves the fact: there are universes infinite in number, each separated from the other by the thinnest of imaginable partitions. Let me show you."

He adjusted several dials and depressed a stud. Parts of the machine lighted up as vacuum tubes warmed rapidly. A soft humming came from it.

"This," he went on, "is a tiny model of the machine that will destroy the Trisz—I should say, that *has* destroyed the Trisz, since *that* future is already determined. I built it to ascertain experimentally the factors I have been telling you about. You will notice this . . ." He pointed toward the heart of the machine, where a tiny violet flame arced continuously between two electrodes.

"That arc is a point of contact between our space-time and another, somewhere among the infinite number of universes that do exist. Semantics breaks down—words become meaningless when we try to describe the existence of these universes. Shall we say that they are on different planes, have varying periods of vibration? Much study will be required to devise an adequate language to express the physical situation.

"However, if I thrust the end of a stylus into the arc—like this," he thrust the instrument into the flame until half its length was swallowed, "it passes through the hole I have made in space-time and emerges in another universe."

The forefront of his audience crowded close. The stylus seemed to end abruptly at the point where it touched the outer influence of the tiny arc. Kor withdrew the stylus, held it up, then inserted it as before.

"Now," he said, "if I change the adjustment of the machine to switch over to still another of the infinite number of existing universes . . ." He turned a dial slowly. The machine howled, and Kor held up the stylus, neatly sliced off at the middle. "The other end of this stylus," he grinned, "was left in the first universe as the influence of the machine was moved to the second."

He called for order at this point, and the Men reluctantly returned to their seats.

"What is the Trisz?" Kor went on. "It is a single, universal being existing in another universe adjacent to our own —and it completely fills that universe! It consists of what we would consider pure energy. In our Universe, the Trisz would be a solid body—matter, not energy.

"The Trisz universe is timeless. Only its excursion into this Universe has made the Trisz aware of time, which it sees as an obstacle to continuity. Time, in its function as the catalyst of awareness, prevents the Trisz from entering our universe completely. The vibratory influence of time allows the Trisz to project itself into this universe only in infinitesimal spurts instead of all at once and everywhere simultaneously. Imagine the Trisz as like the head of a chicken pecking corn, moving rapidly back and forth. It can penetrate into our Universe only during the positive swing of the time-cycle, and must withdraw on the negative.

"We never dared expose our powers in the neighborhood of the Trisz. But only by doing so could the nature of the Trisz be discovered. When I trapped the Trisz in the field of the time-stasis, its true nature became apparent to me. My mind drained the Trisz mind of its entire store of knowledge." Kor tapped his forehead significantly. "Everything the Trisz knows, I know, too—and a few things besides!"

His listeners sat now with bated breath.

"How many parts of the Trisz are in view at one time? Only one . . . the same Trisz is everywhere observable simultaneously. The Trisz is a whole—not a multiplicity of individuals. It simply manifests itself as it wills—subject to the limitations set upon it by the time-element of our Universe.

"The Trisz was born in the airless reaches of interstellar space, and it fed on the radiation of distant suns. As the Trisz grew, it reached out for the stars, swallowed them and drained them of their energy.

"The universe of the Trisz is now cold and dark. The energy of its last sun was long ago drunk by the Trisz. The Trisz became a field of static energy, with nowhere further to grow into. It is aware of its own end, but it cannot know when it will occur because it has no actual appreciation of time. I know what the Trisz' end is . . . and I know when it will occur. That is why I have said that the Trisz has already been destroyed, because its future is absolutely determined—as much as if it had already happened."

"Tell me," said Val Shan. "If the Trisz expansion took place solely in search of energy, why does it bother with the inhabitants of our Universe? Why doesn't it draw energy directly from the stars?"

"The amount of energy required to open a hole in space," Kor returned, "is prodigious. The nature of the Trisz will not permit it to concentrate more than a small portion of its available energy upon creating an opening. And the opening is a very small one—one that could not exist in the frightful force fields of a star. Therefore, the Trisz can draw only enough energy to maintain its interspatial opening."

"From the water stolen from the various planets?" suggested Devon, focusing the stub of his cold cigar into incandescence and puffing furiously.

Kor tapped his thumbnail with the shorn end of the stylus. "From that—and one other source. We have always considered the Trisz in the light of being a more or less human type of conqueror. On the contrary, the Trisz is alien to everything we know.

"Evidence of Trisz killing is not new. We did not know how the Trisz killed, but now we do. The Trisz draws life-energy from its victim and converts it to its own vital kind of energy. The Trisz colonies scattered throughout space? They do not exist! Colonists are recruited to furnish the Trisz with a constant supply of needed life-energy."

Val Shan grimaced. Devon dropped his cigar butt and ground it under foot. He focused on the tip of a fresh cigar and puffed furiously. The assembly of Men rumbled protest.

"Very well," growled Devon. "If the Trisz is bound to be destroyed, I suppose there is nothing further we need do except sit back and wait until the creature goes poof! and vanishes."

"You need not worry about what to do, Doctor," Kor told him seriously. "We shall all be carried along by events as they occur. Our work is cut out for us now, and we can't avoid it." He turned to Val Shan. "Your first move is to call in every Man from the Search Battalions, issue instructions to—"

## 20. FIRE OUT OF HEAVEN

The project Kor Danay put into action called upon the entire manpower and technological resources of the Scarlet Sages. In the cavern cities of Earth, and the other inhabited planets where the Men maintained operations, every mind and machine was turned to the immediate problem.

"Power!" Kor said. "Energy! That is what we are going to need!"

He let them know the gigantic aspect of his plan, what he desired to do and why. Kor stood before the tri-dimensional space viewer in Val Shan's office in Sub-den. His audience consisted of Val Shan and the highest-ranking members of the Men, those who wore the green robes of supreme authority.

Kor adjusted the viewer to his satisfaction. It disclosed a blazing cluster of supernal suns, light-years distant in space.

"Here is an open cluster of stars," Kor pointed out, "about a million parsecs beyond the extreme edge of our galaxy. It contains about five thousand stars, all possessing the same proper motion. As you can see from the nebular remnants connecting the stars, this is a young system in which no living thing has yet developed."

The cluster under discussion glowed with the loveliness of precious stones strewn on a field of black velvet. Filmy strands of nebulosity looped from sun to sun, stood in delicate whorls and silken strands.

"We will harness the energy of these suns—all of them," Kor continued. "I have already explained to you the technique of hurling the Fire out of Heaven—the ancient term being more romantic than descriptive. A similar technique, mechanically applied, will combine the energy of the suns in this cluster, will give us the power we need to penetrate into the universe of the Trisz."

Even as Kor talked, the legions of Men labored at the task. Dark stars in the cluster . . . great masses of matter huger than planets, but cold, solidified, served as power bases. From a hundred planets of the galaxy, a stream of material was being transmitted instantaneously through sub-space to permanent locations on those utterly airless and lightless worlds. Fantastic towers, bolstered and braced against the prodigious force of gravitation they had to combat, climbed into blazing-starred skies, stood as skeletal silhouettes against the drooping folds of nebulosity that glowingly spanned the firmament.

No such task could have been performed in secret. The Sages threw off their mask of secrecy. Their hidden cities everywhere erected titanic force fields for protection against attacks by the Trisz that might mature at any hour. On Earth, the Sages were recalled from the Chapters. The situation was explained to the Blue Brotherhood, and as many as possible were transported bodily to the subterranean cities of the Men. The transition was performed smoothly.

But as quickly as the Men acted, the Trisz awoke to the realization of danger. Flying squads moved in on the Lodges, and though the scarlet-clad Men escaped, many of the Blue Brotherhood were taken.

Val Shan told Kor about the fate of Blue Brother Set; he had not been one of those to escape the thrust of the Trisz.

On a thousand worlds, within the galaxy, closest to the field of the Men's operation, a Trisz combat fleet was shaping. Triszmen throughout the Universe labored to build a fleet that would destroy the installations the Men were building in the open cluster.

A patrol of Men numbering thousands covered the vast reach of extra-galactic space in and around the star cluster. Their minds were interlocked, spread in a vast screen encompassing trillions of cubic miles of space, to prevent the materialization of the Trisz interspatial penetration within the cluster.

But no such defense could avail against the mental power of the Trisz wielded over its slaves. They labored till they dropped, forging new weapons to arm the fleet.

Kor worked feverishly on a giant world a hundred times the diameter of Earth. The great mass of its bulk set up strains in space itself, caused a thousand delays, presented a ceaseless stream of special problems, in readying the equipment. And just before the power-network was finished, the Trisz struck.

Important as Kor's place was on the job, he and he alone could face the Trisz fleet and gain for the racing Men the time they needed to complete the power circuit. Kor left the job in the hands of capable assistants and fled into space.

Space swarmed invisibly with the Men of the outpost patrols. Kor felt their presence everywhere as his mind lashed out in the vacuity of cold. His senses received a thousand reports at once that enabled him to beam his pereceptions directly toward the oncoming fleet.

The enemy was as uncountable as the stars in the Milky Way. Grains of sand in the remote depths of space, they hung like a cloud swept on the wings of an incredible wind.

Kor's mind was filled with the high whistles of the Trisz-note, as he palped the plunging ships. He sensed the crews of human, humanoid, and bizarre life forms pressed into service by the Trisz. In every vessel, the Trisz was present, a curious multiplicity of its single self, commanding, directing operations, laying plans for the assault upon the gigantic worlds of the Men.

Kor linked his mind with the thousands who patrolled. He remembered with amusement his first experiments with hurling the Fire. To have linked his mind then with another would have been dangerous. It was different now, thanks to his new understanding of the infinite orders of rationalization.

Kor felt a curious, floating aloneness as he cast out the time-stasis field and his conscious self hovered free of the reaction he set in motion.

Three light-years away, a sun of the great cluster erupted violently. Flames whorled on its surface, shot upward with dizzying speed and vanished into the darksome funnel of sub-space Kor created there. It would take three years for the blazing incandescence of that nova-like explosion to reach Kor's position—but he knew that it happened, and he knew when it winked suddenly out, though its ghost-image continued to blaze, and would continue so as its last departing radiation trailed for three long years through space.

Like a broad fan of luminescence, clawed and fanged with the unleashed energy of a giant sun, the nova appeared in space ahead of Kor, between him and the light-years distant fleet. It spread slowly, seemingly gelid in the frigid non-temperature of space.

Another sun erupted violently in the cluster, was sucked into the sub-space funnel, and appeared lashing in the neighborhood of its brother sun, fanning out into the depths of space at the rate of millions of miles a second. That automaton of Kor's divisible mind worked automatically, hurling sun after sun toward the approaching fleet, until all of space was a seething magnetic storm beyond description, through which no material thing could pass. Fleet as the ships of the Trisz were, it would take them six months to draw to a slow halt, alter their course, and bypass the deadly barrier.

Kor returned to his interrupted labors on the planet.

"That will hold them long enough," he communicated to Val Shan. "I didn't have the heart to manifest those suns within the fleet. Those poor slaves are not to blame. As soon as our work here is finished, the Trisz will vanish from every one of those ships and the crews will be free of its influence. They will be glad enough to return to their home bases."

The work went on under the cold light of the stars. Kor himself brought the last wire into position, welded it in place.

Val Shan looked worriedly into his eyes. "We have done everything possible? You are certain now?"

Kor nodded.

"Yes. It is time now for the Men to withdraw to the galaxy. The drain of energy will destroy space itself throughout this sector. I want none other here than myself."

"Remember," Val Shan reminded him, "your new body lies in a vault in Sub-den. Atom for atom, it is identical with this body whose hand I clasp. When your work is done in the Trisz universe, return to us."

Kor Danay smiled grimly.

The Scarlet Sages, in a single surge, vanished from the region of the star-cluster. Alone on the vast, darksome world wheeling in the midst of nebulosity, Kor prepared himself for the final act of his drama. The machine towered on a glassy, obsidian plain. This was the control center of the vast network of sub-etheric connections from world to world and star to star. The power of thousands of suns was linked here in this great machine that lifted lofty ramparts above the plain.

Quickly, Kor flitted across the vast control board, checking and adjusting the settings of dials and verniers. He had not left this final setting to a subordinate. Too much depended upon accuracy. He placed himself in the operator's niche, a thousand feet above the plain, where shortly the violet arc of the dimension-penetrator would build itself into a ram of power that would punch a hole in space and time and let the enormous energy of this cluster of stars pour through the rent into the universe of the Trisz.

Everything was in readiness. Kor strapped himself in the operator's niche with a silent prayer. Nothing could go wrong now. The Sage expanded his mind, felt it spring out, unwinding like a lash of steel, establishing the necessary contacts. His conscious mind floated free, aware that his physical self yanked a lever. The metal bar slid smoothly into place without a click in the airless void. For an instant, the wheeling Universe stood still—then all was dark, cold, and intensely silent.

No more could he perceive the glowing nebulosity of the wandering system, nor its thousands of glowing suns, like great arcs in the frosted sky.

The space of a vibrating electron away, his own Universe still existed, still blazed with the starry incandescence of its firmament. But the stars of the wandering cluster were dark, drained of their energy to the ultimate erg, lightless, lifeless—utterly destroyed. The great machine among them on that frigid world Kor had left was a mass of molten metal, already congealing around the material body of the Man Kor. And throughout all of that Universe Kor Danay's mind had left, the Trisz vanished, cast out forever by that mortal thrust.

There was a flutter in the dark of his consciousness, a breathless stir of something that drew Kor's perception to a razor edge. His mind still expanded, flinging its influence ever outward into the universe and the encompassing energy-body of the Trisz. There were worlds here that had once been planets, and worlds that had once been suns, cold now and dead, forever wheeling in the empty dark, empty save for the frictionless fluid of the Trisz' being.

And something else was here. Kor paused to wonder. A whisper, a stir, a rustling call.

"Soma!" he cried. "Soma! I hear you!"

Now was the moment! The Sage unleashed the flood of energy he bore. The time-stasis field leaped out, slowly at first, then faster and faster—faster than thought in the timeless reaches of this universe. The Trisz universe accelerated. Awareness grew in every atom and circling electron. Energy strained against energy within the body of the Trisz as the alien monster died. Supertitanic forces weaved from end to end of the universe, lashed with demoniacal fury. The universe was a silent blaze of wondrous light. Softly, Kor Danay called out in the silence of his mind: "Soma!"

*"Kor! The Universe lives—because of you."*

Before the light dimmed in his consciousness he thought, "There is a place for us, too!"

128